# AMONG THE QUIET FOLKS

# AMONG THE QUIET FOLKS

# FOLKS

## JOHN MOORE

ALAN SUTTON
1986

Alan Sutton Publishing Limited
17a Brunswick Road
Gloucester GL1 1HG

First published in the United States 1967
First published in the United Kingdom 1984
Reprinted 1986

Moore, John, *1907–1967*
  Among the quiet folks.
  I. Title    II. Series
  823'.914[F]    PR6025.0572

  ISBN 0-86299-146-3

*Cover picture: detail from* Harvest Time *by George Vicat Cole.*
Bristol City Art Gallery.

Printed and bound in Great Britain.

*To My Friend*
*Nicholas Monsarrat*

# CONTENTS

# AMONG THE QUIET FOLKS

# Among the Quiet Folks

*The child watched her father sharpening his scythe. Her* eyes turning to and fro could hardly follow the swift movement of the whetstone. Her father had stood the scythe upside down so that its heel was level with his chin. His wrist flicked deftly as he stroked the blade with the stone. Long practice enabled him to do this without looking; he spoke over his shoulder towards the cottage behind him:

"I be going to have a day with them as can't answer back."

"Then take the brat with you, for goodness!"

"She'll be all right playing in the garden."

"She never do play. She just hangs around. Gets on my nerves."

It seemed to the child that the whetstone shrieked in imitation of her mother's voice.

"Why they wants half-term at Whitsun beats me. What for do we pay them teachers——"

"The likes of us don't have to pay 'em."

"Well, somebody do. And what do we get for it? They ain't taught *her* much, for goodness——"

"Not in front of Emily——"

"That kid ain't right. Ars't her what she was doing just now and she said, *Thinking*. Well!"

"Emily," said her father, arresting his right hand in the middle of a stroke; and because her mother had fallen silent too, it was as if the whole world went still suddenly. "Like to come along o' me, have a day among the Quiet Folks?"

She knew what he meant. It was what he always said when the Vicar asked him to mow the long grass in the churchyard: "A day among the Quiet Folks," who didn't gossip nor chatter nor nag, nag, nag.

He took her hand and slung the scythe over his shoulder, and they went down the short village street between the thatched houses. through the lych-gate, into the silent acre of grass and of graves.


For a while she was content to watch the green swath falling. It was still dewy, and sweet-smelling; she heaped it up to make tumps, which she burrowed in, and pretended she was some kind of animal that lived in such tumps. Every few minutes her father paused and made the stone sing against the blade; its keen edge when he started again made a *swish* so soft it was like a sigh. Here and there were clumps of nettles—'ettles as he called them: They troublesome 'ettles, how they do grow. When the scythe met them it made a rougher, rasping sound. Old mossy tombstones appeared where the nettles had stood, and he trimmed the herbage neatly round them. Sometimes he bent down and tried to read the words on a tombstone; and he would talk to himself: "Annie Elizabeth, 1757, R.I.P. *You* bin quiet these two hundred years." Then he would straighten himself, and re-light his pipe, and stand looking up at the tall church spire. Emily had a sense of his easiness as he stood there, and they smiled at each other, which they never did at home.

But soon she grew tired of watching him, and of the game with the grass tumps, and she crept away, through the soft, tickling grass and the moon-daisies that stood higher than her waist. She remembered something her father had said about the Quiet Folks "pushing up the daisies," and she fancied the flowers were taller wherever there was a stone. She tried to imagine how the dead people pushed them up, but she couldn't understand it, how they could do such a thing when they were dead. She explained it to herself in terms of magic—the Quiet Folks *wished,* and the daisies grew. The idea pleased her, and she began to feel familiar with the Quiet Folks and close to them. She observed the different monuments which marked their habitations, and before long a large white Angel engaged her attention. Its wings were spread wide as if it were about to fly, or perhaps as if it had only just landed. It was the tallest thing in the churchyard, and Emily made a bee-line towards it. The grave, she soon saw, was quite a new one, and there were flowers on it, as well as a holly wreath with a label which said *In loving memory of Auntie.* The name on the headstone caught Emily's eye, and it was one you couldn't forget if you had ever heard it: PENELOPE PRENDERGAST. At once she remembered Mrs. Prendergast who had lived in the big house at the top of the village, and Mrs. Prendergast's Corgi dog which she dragged round on a lead, jerking the lead viciously to hurt its neck every time it looked at a lamp-post. She remembered the terror of meeting Mrs. Prendergast, who looked like an old witch and who hated all children because she thought they might damage the

flowers in her garden, when they crept in to look for lost
balls. Even if you hadn't done anything wrong she would
stop you and stare at you in her peaky way and say:

"Whose little girl are you?"

"Emily Radford."

"Well, your mother wouldn't like you going about with
your knees all filthy. You've been climbing over walls, I
daresay. Going where you shouldn't. Go home and clean
yourself. Tell Mrs. Radford I said so."

Once Emily did tell her, and her mother said: "The
old bitch."

Emily now remembered the hearse going by, on a Saturday morning in March. She remembered it because of the
flowers—they were piled up all over the coffin so that it
seemed as if Mrs. Prendergast was taking her whole garden
with her on her last ride, in case the boys should do harm
to it! Behind the hearse, in a big car, sat two sharp-faced
women in black. They both held handkerchiefs and dabbed
at their eyes. Emily's mother, leaning over the garden-gate,
had said, "Crocodile tears . . . They comes into sixty thousand." She had a mop in her hand, and she spun it round
and sent the dirty water flying as if to show that she didn't
care tuppence about Mrs. Prendergast in her coffin. "Well,
*she* won't trouble no one no more," said Emily's mother,
as the bare-headed men carried the coffin through the lych-
gate.

With difficulty and some bewilderment, crouching in the
shadow of the Angel's wings, Emily now read the inscription
upon the stone. (The Angel, barefooted, stood upon this
stone. It had toenails just like a human being.) The inscription ran:

In Fond Remembrance of Penelope Prendergast of this Parish, whose Christian

PIETY, KINDLINESS AND COMPASSION FOR BOTH
MAN AND BEAST, AS WELL AS HER BENEFACTIONS
TO THE SICK AND THE POOR, WERE AN EXAMPLE
TO ALL WHO KNEW HER. SHE FELL ASLEEP ON
THE 15TH OF MARCH 1964 AGED 73 YEARS. R.I.P.

Emily read it three times, and was deeply troubled by it,
for she kept seeing Mrs. Prendergast jerking her dog's head
and waving her stick at little boys playing ball-games near
her gate. As she strove to get the sense of the inscription,
she became aware—as she was often aware—of the terrifying
nature of the grown-up world, with all its contradictions and
perplexities. In sudden fear of it she withdrew herself as
a snail draws back its horns into its shell. She shut her mind
alike to the words on the headstone and to the memory
of the old woman with the dog. She fell into a daydream,
wondering why there were no moon-daisies round Mrs. Prendergast's tomb. Perhaps she hadn't *wished,* down there under the earth; perhaps she couldn't; more likely she wouldn't,
out of sheer ill-temper. Idly glancing about her, Emily was
struck by something unfriendly, even menacing, in the attitude of the Angel. It looked as if it were about to pounce,
to swoop down on Emily because she trespassed there. Its
face, which was pointed and peaky, reminded her of Mrs.
Prendergast's, and she was indeed persuaded that it was
a likeness of Mrs. Prendergast turned into an Angel. Warily
she began to crawl backwards, on her knees, because she
was reluctant to turn her back on it. Thus she retreated
until she was in the long grass; and feeling fairly safe there,
but not quite safe, she got up and ran until she came to
the very edge of the churchyard. There she happened to
stub her shins against a very small tombstone which was
hidden by the grasses: and being out of breath from running
she lay down before it.

She was listening to the corncrake sound of her father's whetstone, and watching a bumblebee furry with pollen burrowing into a flower, and forgetting about Mrs. Prendergast, when she realized, with the utmost dismay, that the name on the little tombstone was her own. All the letters weren't there, for it was an old stone, smoothed by the weather: but she could make out E M—then there was a blank space—L and part of a Y. For a moment this terrified her; then she assured herself that there were other people with the same name—no less than three girls at school were called Emily—so she crept nearer to the stone, wriggling on her tummy until she was lying along the narrow hump just in front of it. She parted the grasses and now she could read quite easily what it said on the stone, for the slanting sun etched each letter with a black shadow. *Here lyeth,* she read, *EM LY beloved child of John and Jane Nott, who dyed of the smallpox at her Aunt Catchmay's in Gloster on Christmas Day 1720 in the 8th yr. of her age . . .* There was some more writing after that, but the moss at the bottom of the stone had covered up several of the letters. She spelt them out as best she could:

AFT R  LIF 'S  FITFU  FEV    SHE  SL  PS  WELL.

Emily began to feel it was important that she should make out the meaning of the words. They tantalised her; and at last, puzzling over them, she achieved an inspired guess at "sleeps well." This feat she promptly chalked up in her mind as a small triumph over her mother, who had declared only this morning, "They ain't taught *her* much . . . That kid ain't right." Murmuring to herself over and over again the three words, "She sleeps well," Emily had a powerful impression of the everlasting quietude in which the other Emily dwelt. At the same time she discovered, with

much awe and a little misgiving, that her own body exactly
fitted the grassy ridge on which she was lying. She pressed
her toes into the bottom of the hump and her face into the
cool, moss-grown bit at the top of it; it was made exactly to
her measure. This gave her an extraordinary feeling of
closeness to her namesake, and before long her dismay vanished, and she put her mouth to the earth and breathed,
"I'm an Emily too." She wondered why they had put this
child so far away from the other graves, and tears came into
her eyes as she thought of the loneliness of Emily. She
wanted to give her some comfort, so she picked a handful
of moon-daisies and laid them neatly along the top of the
hump; but they didn't look very impressive when she remembered the white carnations and lilies-of-the-valley on
Mrs. Prendergast's grave. A daring project formed in her
mind, and she could feel her heart beating against the earth
as she whispered, "I'll fetch you some proper flowers." She
jumped up and ran back towards the Angel. At first she
ran very fast, but as she approached it she slowed down to a
trot, then to a walk, and at last she stopped altogether. She
began to wish she hadn't promised the flowers to Emily;
for the Angel was looking straight at her, peering very much
as Mrs. Prendergast had peered, and the Angel's arms were
stretched over the flowers in an attitude which seemed to say,
"You *dare* touch them!"

Emily edged nearer, one step at a time, until at the very
brink of the grave her resolution failed her and she drew
back; perhaps she would have run away then, but she heard
her father at the other side of the churchyard sharpening
his scythe, and the familiar sound gave her a brief sense
of security. In that moment she dashed forward, seized the
flowers, and bore them away. Scarcely feeling the prickly
thistles and the hot nettles against her knees, she did not
pause until she came to Emily's grave; she laid the carnations

at its head and the lilies at its foot. She knelt down and smelt the clove scent of the one bunch, the sweetness of the other, and the thought that Emily could not smell them moved her to pity. With love and tenderness she rearranged the flowers, and suddenly the sense of a mysterious communion overcame her, so that her heart seemed to be filled simultaneously with happiness and terror. She lay down by the grave and she wept a little, but they were not the kind of tears that hurt. They dried at once when she heard her father shouting, "Em'ly, Em'ly—where's that brat got to?" and she stayed only long enough to whisper into the green moss, "I'll come back some day, I'll come back soon." Then she ran to her father, and she noticed how different the churchyard looked—the sun as it sank towards the hills made the swaths of mown grass like small waves on the sea, and all the tombstones were like jagged black rocks standing up among them.

Her father said, "Where you bin, kid?" but he didn't wait for an answer; he was grumbling about his back: "Hard mowing, I'd like that fat parson to try it, half a crown a blessed hour." Then he said he wasn't going to do the bit round the edges and Emily was glad, because nobody could see the little grave while the grass stood round it, and the flowers would remain a secret between her and the child who had died on Christmas Day. Her father slung the scythe over his shoulder, and Emily fell in beside him, and as they went up the village street her father said, "Ah well, 'twas a change to spend an hour or two with them as don't answer you back."

Next day was Sunday, and the church bells were ringing, so that her mother said, "I wish they'd shut up, banging and clanging; what rights have they got? S'pose I was to

shove on the wireless loud as that they'd have me for disturbing the neighbours." Then she did put on the wireless,
as loud as she could, partly to spite the bellringers and
partly because she wanted to hear the music while she was
Hoovering.

Emily's father said something about Bedlam and bicycled
off to his allotment; Emily slipped out and went down to
the churchyard, but because of all the cars outside she dared
not go in. She lurked by the lych-gate and listened to the
organ playing in the church and the gabbling noise of people
trying to catch up with long sentences as they sang the
Psalms. Later she watched the congregation coming out.
She saw two women go across the grass to Mrs. Prendergast's
grave, and she recognised them as the two who had sat in
the car behind the flower-filled hearse. She remembered
what her mother had said about them, but she hadn't known
what it meant; she thought of them, however, as the Crocodile Women. As they approached the grave they pointed
and became suddenly agitated, and of course Emily realized
that they were missing the flowers. They stood under the
Angel, and seemed to argue, and shook their heads. Then
they walked away, and they passed quite close to Emily
Nott's little grave without noticing it.

It pleased Emily to think of the flowers lying there unseen,
a secret shared between her and the other Emily.

In the afternoon she returned, but there was a Confir-
mation; she watched the fussy parents hurrying along their
girls in white dresses, their boys with scrubbed faces and
specially brushed hair. Still she was afraid to go into the
churchyard and she was curiously troubled by the thought
of Emily's loneliness.

On Monday, because it was Bank Holiday, there were
more cars than ever. Crowds of people were visiting the old

church, and five red charabancs stood outside the White
Lion, which was nearly opposite. Emily walked on down
the lane as far as the river and picked some flowers for her
friend and namesake, yellow flags and tall pink things and
one water lily which she hooked out of the water with a
stick. She nearly fell in, and got her dress muddy, so that
when she went back to the churchyard and looked over the
wall, she could imagine Mrs. Prendergast peering at her
through the eyes of the Angel: "Go home and tell your
mother to clean you up. Tell her I said so."

She did go home, because there were still too many people
about. She felt about the little grave as she imagined a bird
must feel about its nest: she must not allow herself to be
seen going towards it.

The flowers had faded in her hot hand; but her mother,
seeing them, guessed she'd been down to the river, which
was forbidden. She spat on a handkerchief and scrubbed
her knees, and while she was doing so suddenly lifted up
her skirt and smacked her bottom. Then she sent her to
bed. Lying there still and sullen, Emily was remembering
that there were some new, white flowers on Mrs. Prendergast's grave. She had seen them when she looked over the
wall, and she was thinking that the Crocodile Women must
have put them there; they were very grand-looking flowers,
and she was coveting them for Emily.

On Tuesday afternoon (for it was still the half-term holiday) she found the churchyard deserted, and only the
pigeons on the church roof saw her as she darted from the
lych-gate to Mrs. Prendergast's grave and stole a large
bunch of white gladioli off it. The magnificence of the
snowy spray gave her an undue sense of victory over the
detested Angel, and on the spur of the moment she did

something dreadful. She cocked a snook at it; and was immediately ashamed, terrified, and convinced that she would
be punished for what she had done. In chastened mood she
went to the little grave and laid the white flowers upon it;
but her foolish act had robbed her of the pleasure she would
otherwise have got from bringing so princely a gift to Emily.
Then she saw the Vicar, with his tummy bulging under a
black cassock, striding down the path towards the church
door. She thought of him as a possible instrument of the
Angel's revenge, so she lay down and hid among the grasses
on the grave; and there it seemed her punishment crept
upon her, for her head began to ache, she felt sick, and
shivers ran up and down her spine. She got up at last and
tottered home, and as soon as she went into the back room
her mother pounced on her:

"Look at you, all flushed and dopey, took sick, have you;
it's getting in the river done it; you been down there again,
I daresay—good mind to give you a hiding." But she didn't
give her a hiding. Upstairs in the bedroom undressing her,
she exclaimed:

"Goodness, look at that, well I never did." There were
small pink spots all over Emily's body from her waist down
to her thighs, and across her back too—she saw them in the
looking-glass while her mother went downstairs for a hot-
water bottle. They itched all the more after she'd seen them,
and she scratched wildly, so that she left the marks of her
nails. Her headache was like a hammer thumping within her
skull. She thought that she was going to die and that it had
something to do with the Angel.

Tucked into bed, she cuddled the hot-water bottle, and
the world drifted away from her; she saw letters before her
eyes, FITFUFEV, and was troubled by them. Now and then
her mother's face appeared, unfamiliarly kind, and her

mother's hand stroked her forehead. A night light was lit
and it cast huge shadows like Angel's wings. Her father's
voice spoke out of these shadows, half laughing and surprising
her because of the laughter in it just as she was going to die.
"All the kids has it: *chicken pox.*" The last syllable stuck
in her mind and awakened a memory of the writing on the
tombstone: "Dyed of the smallpox . . . Christmas Day . . ."
She must have spoken the last words aloud, for her father's
voice said:

"No, child, it's six months to Christmas."

Her mother's voice:

"She's dreaming. Look how she tosses and turns."

Emily heard them tiptoe out. She heard the door close.
Fever, she said to herself. FITFUFEVER. The letters danced
before her again, but this time it was like one of those
puzzles which they had given her to do at school, what
they called an I.Q. test—the girls said it was to find out if
you were a loonie. Gradually the puzzle began to resolve
itself, AFTER LIF' S, AFTER LIFE'S—then suddenly she had
it, all except one letter: AFTER LIFE'S FITFU  FEVER SHE
SLEEPS WELL.

It was quite clear in her mind for a moment, and she saw
the words etched by sunlight on the tombstone under the
name EM LY. Half-way between waking and sleeping, she
began to talk to herself: "Em ly Nott," she said, "Em ly
Nott, Em ly is not." It struck her as funny and she laughed
aloud. Then the door opened and her parents were beside
the bed.

"What's the matter, child?"

"Emily is not. I am."

"It's the fever."

"I am. She's not but I am. I am Emily Am."

"Try to lie quiet, child . . . Better tomorrow . . . *Sleep
well.*"

This time she didn't hear them go out. She slipped imperceptibly into a dream, and she was smelling the wet earth, she was lying side by side with Emily Nott and at last she knew what Emily Nott looked like: she had carroty hair and a very pale skin with freckles. She loved her, and held her hand for comfort as they lay together. She was looking at the freckles on Emily Nott's nose, and then she suddenly realised that she was looking at herself, as if in a looking-glass. The freckles became pink spots. And now she didn't know whether it was she or Emily Nott lying in the earth, Emily Nott or Emily Am, or both of them together. The spots became enormous, they swelled and swelled until they covered all the nose and the cheeks and the eyes, and then there was no face at all, and the dream faded, and she slept well.

The nightmare had been so vivid that the first thing she did, when she woke in the morning, was to jump out of bed and look at herself in the glass; she was thankful to find that she still had cheeks and eyes and a nose. Indeed, there were no spots on her face at all; and the ones on her tummy were still only pinhead size. Her headache had gone, and she no longer thought she was dying. Within two days the spots changed to little water blisters rather like tear-drops, and she scratched them off with satisfaction. Scabs formed, and her mother put woolly socks over her hands, tying them at the wrists. Then, on a warm day. Emily was allowed to play in the sun; but because she was still infectious she mustn't go to school.

Seizing an opportunity when her mother was out, Emily made her way down to the churchyard, filched a bunch of rather faded white roses off Mrs. Prendergast's grave, and took them as tribute to Emily Nott. But this time an alarming thing happened. She was on her way out of the churchyard when suddenly a man rose up out of the ground in front of her. It was just like a picture of the Resurrection she had seen in church; and she screamed. The man, however, laughed; and Emily saw that he had a spade and was digging a hole for some new dead person.

"Made you jump," said the man. "Well, you mind I don't pop you in it, 'stead of old Butcher Barnes as pegged out a-Toosdy."

Emily remembered Butcher Barnes, who was very fat with bulging red arms. You could hardly tell them from the meat when he was cutting it; and she thought it would be a squash if he were going into that narrow hole. But of course it wasn't finished yet; the man set to work again chopping at the edges with his spade. Emily ran away; and she was glad he hadn't seen her carrying the flowers. She had realised by now that there was an element of danger in what she was doing; and oddly enough this pleased her, for there seemed something sacrificial in running a risk on behalf of Emily.

The memory of her nightmare had mostly faded; the horror of it hadn't outlasted the spots on her tummy. But a trace of it remained imprinted on her mind as the scab marks stayed on her body; and this mere shadow of a recollection gave her an added sense of closeness to the child in the ground. She saw Emily Nott as a little girl like herself, pale skin, freckles, carroty hair and all; she had become almost as real as someone you held hands with. She was also aware, though she couldn't have put it into words, of having shared with Emily Nott a profound and awful experience. Her illness, she thought, had been the same as Emily's: Fitfufever, poxiness. But Emily Nott had died—leaving behind the Christmas holly and mistletoe and the new toys on her bed—whereas she had survived, she was Emily Am. She began to think of herself most of the time

as Emily Am; and when she laid the roses on the grave she
had whispered, "Emily Am here," and it was like sharing a
joke.

She believed that the flowers in some way might make up
to Emily Nott for the Christmas presents unopened, the
bulging stocking unexplored.

So within two or three days she went again to the churchyard; but this time she dared not go in, for the Crocodile
Women were walking round and round the Angel, and
with them was the fat Vicar. She crouched behind the hedge
and tried to hear what they were saying. The only word
she heard was "Poltergeist." It was repeated two or three
times. The Vicar laughed and said, "Poltergeist with two
legs, I'm sure." She didn't like the sound of that; it had
the implication of some horrible, hornéd, long-toothed,
ravening Thing.

Then the Vicar and the Crocodile Women moved out
of earshot.


"Sacrilege," one of the women was saying, "That's what
it is. Sacrilege."

"Well, I'd hardly go so far . . . ," said the Vicar. Sacrilege,
he supposed, would have to happen inside a church. Perhaps
you could call it petty larceny? Both women bridled at that.

"Petty, indeed!"

"Well, I'm afraid I've got a Churchwardens' Meeting . . ."
The Vicar disliked these nieces almost as much as he had
disliked Mrs. Prendergast herself. He loathed churchyard
Angels and he particularly disliked the ostentatious one
they had put up in memory of Mrs. P. He could have forbidden it, but that would have caused a fuss, and he was
an easy-going man. He often invited nice, cheerful old
ladies to madeira cake and madeira wine after the service

on Sunday, shortening his sermon to allow plenty of time before lunch. But he never invited the Misses Prendergast. Indeed no! He knew exactly why they had put up that expensive Angel and why they had composed that guff about Mrs. Prendergast's goodness to man and beast. It was because they were superstitious, and still frightened of Mrs. Prendergast. They thought she might do them some harm, even from beyond the grave, if they did not pay proper tribute to her. She might, for instance, give them diseases; or cause their shares to go down. That was why, although they 'only put threepence in the plate, they laid costly flowers every week upon her grave—like poor ignorant blacks placating the spirits of their ancestors. (The Vicar, over his port in the evening, sometimes read *The Golden Bough*.)

"Heathens," he grunted to himself, as he hurried towards the Vestry (although of course he hadn't *really* got a Church-wardens' Meeting).

The Misses Prendergast, walking back towards the lych-gate, were saying:

"Some *special* flowers. Bait. Arum lilies. Bait the trap. Keep watch."

But Emily didn't hear them. She was still hiding behind the hedge, and she nearly jumped out of her skin when they suddenly appeared and saw her crouching there.

"What on earth . . . Come here, child, what are you doing?" said the taller.

"N-nothing," said Emily. Then she added swiftly, "Looking for birds' nests"—for indeed she had found a black-bird's in that hedge.

"You ought to know better," said this Crocodile Woman, who talked just like Mrs. Prendergast. "Stealing the poor thing's eggs—" though Emily had said nothing about eggs.

Muttering, the Crocodile Women walked away. They knew she could hear so they spelt out words, as if that would prevent her from understanding. "S–o–f–t," said the one Crocodile.

"It's interbreeding" said the other. "The schoolmistress was telling me some of the children are almost——"

"What?"

"M–e–n–t–a–l."

Next day was the last before Emily went back to school. It seemed very important that she should replace the faded roses and explain to Emily Nott why she wouldn't be able to visit her very often. But she had a keen sense of danger, rather pleasurable, as she made her way down to the church-yard. The church bell was tolling gloomily; at noon, she'd overheard her mother saying they were going to put Butcher Barnes under the ground.

"The old meanie," said her mother. "*He* won't fill no more sausages with bread."

What Emily had to do must be done quickly.

She slipped through the lych-gate and ducked low so that the grasses almost hid her, as she ran towards Mrs. Prendergast's grave.

The Angel's hands looked ready to clutch her; she could see the sky between the spread fingers. "You dare!" She hated the Angel, and her hatred gave her courage. Even without it she could never have resisted those great, creamy-soft flowers lying so temptingly upon the grass. Four, five, six of them, like great white cups, each with a yellow spike sticking up in the middle of it. She had never seen such things before; and she thought they were the most beautiful flowers in the world. She instinctively recognised their *sickroom* quality. Their paleness and langour made them

as it were the special property of the dying and the dead.
Emily Nott should have held them to her bosom, to match
her pale cheeks. Emily Nott, lying under the ground, should
have them now, a belated recompense.

She bent down swiftly and picked up the flowers. She
looked round about to make sure that no one was watching
her. The sad, thoughtful-looking yews stood round like
people, but there was no human being in sight. Nevertheless, Emily played the trick which she had learned from
the nesting peewits in the field by the river: she didn't
go straight towards Emily's grave—indeed, she walked for
a little way in the opposite direction. Then she began to
zigzag warily towards it. She had a sense of being watched;
but she put that down to the yew-trees standing sentinel
all round the churchyard.

The arum lilies, cradled in her arms, felt much heavier
than familiar flowers, as if they were made of something
silken or velvety, richer and rarer than petal-stuff. She
touched them, and they had a strange baby-skin softness.
She stared in wonder at the yellow tongues within them.

Then the shout—it was more like a screech—froze her
limbs and seemed, for a moment, even to stop her heart
beating. It wasn't just an ordinary shout; there was a dreadful crow of triumph in it. She ascribed it at first to the
Angel; and turning round in terror, she saw the Angel's
hands pointing towards her. She knew the shout concerned
herself, for it had the quality of a View Halloo: the way
people had shouted at the foxes when her father took her
to see the cubhunting. Like one of those cubs, she doubled
back in her tracks; then she saw a black-clad figure step
out from behind a yew-tree—it was as if the tree itself had
moved—and turned again, bewildered, only to see another
figure emerge from behind another yew. This one held

out its arms as if to shoo her back; she recognised it, and knew that the Crocodile Women were after her. She fled wildly, still clutching the flowers, and tried to hide herself in the long grass. More shouts followed her. Suddenly a hole yawned before her feet and she fell or jumped—she wasn't sure which—into the grave which the man had been digging yesterday. The lilies were crushed beneath her, and gave out a queer, rancid smell. She heard the voice of a Crocodile Woman saying, "This way."

She lay still and tried not to breathe. A few moments later the other Crocodile Woman said, "Where can she have got to?" She raised herself up and peeped out of the grave. She saw the Vicar come out of the church. He was dressed up like he always was on Sundays. One of the Crocodile Women ran to him. They talked. The Vicar shook his head, and pointed up the village street. Then, rather reluctantly, he walked across the short grass beside the Crocodile Woman. The other woman joined them. They were coming towards Emily. When they reached the long grass, they spread out like the beaters she'd watched when the Squire had a shooting party. They quartered the ground, until they were so close that Emily dared not look out any more. She crouched at the bottom of the grave and heard the sound of their feet brushing through the grass as they came nearer. All the time the bell was tolling from the church tower.

Even amid her fear she felt her kinship with Emily Nott. This was the kind of place *she* inhabited. It had a wet smell. At the bottom it was rough with bits of stone. On the sides (as Emily looked up) there was first a layer of yellowish chalk. Near the top there was very dark brown soil, with roots in it. Daisy roots? It was possible to see how the Quiet Folks could push up the daisies, *wishing* away right at the roots of them. Turning over on her back, Emily looked at some tall moon-daisies, slanting over the edge of the grave. A little wind stirred them. Suddenly she saw a boot. It crushed the moon-daisies. The Vicar stood over her, enormous, and with a strange surprise she saw grey flannel trousers underneath his surplice and cassock.

"Well," he said. "Well. Well I never."

Then she heard the quick breaths and the small, excited cries of the Crocodile Women as they approached. In a second they too were standing above her, and she had a jumbled impression of grey stockings and thick black drawers under the black skirts, of peaky faces against the sky, long noses and flared nostrils seen from below . . .

The Vicar was saying urgently:

"They're just coming . . . wouldn't like the relatives to see . . . *decorum* . . ."

He leaned down towards Emily and stretched out his hand.

"Come out, child," he said quite kindly.

Emily took his hand, fat and soft with rings on it. He lifted her out, and then the Crocodile Women saw the flowers. They almost screeched.

"There they are . . . She had them, you see . . . Look, all broken, the beautiful flowers."

They seized Emily's arms, one Crocodile Woman on each side of her. The Vicar murmured:

"Be gentle with her. Strange fantasies of childhood . . . We cannot understand."

One of the Crocodile Women said:

"What's your name, little girl?"

Emily knew that she was putting on a kind voice in front of the Vicar: but at the same time she was deliberately digging her thumbnail into Emily's arm.

Perhaps it was because this hurt so much, or because she was so frightened and confused, that Emily blurted out: "Emily Am."

"Ham?" said the Crocodile Woman. "Ham?"

"No, no," said the Vicar. "She's the little Radford girl from just up the road."

"She said Ham," insisted the Crocodile Woman. Her sister snapped:

"Cunning, you see. Even giving a false name," and dug her thumbnail in deeper.

"Some childish foolishness. She meant no harm. You didn't mean any harm, Emily, did you?" The Vicar smiled at her, and then suddenly, as if he'd pressed a button to change his expression, his face went very solemn and he began to walk away, with his hands folded across his chest. Following him with her eyes, Emily saw the top-hats in the road outside the churchyard, and as if at a signal all the top-hats were removed, and then she saw the men carrying the box. There were flowers on it, but not so many as there had been on Mrs. Prendergast's.

The Vicar walked towards the bearers, with his head bowed and the sun shining on the bald top of it.

The Crocodile Women began to tug her arms, and in their anxiety to get out of sight of the funeral party they dragged her between them through the long grass at the edge of the churchyard. They were making straight for the grave of Emily Nott. Of course they did not know about it, you couldn't see it because of the grass; so although Emily could tell to a foot where the tombstone was, she averted her eyes and looked hard in the opposite direction lest she should help the Crocodile Women to find it and let them see the faded roses on the tump.

"Why did you steal the flowers?"

Emily didn't answer.

"Why did you steal them?"

"Why?" "Why?" "Why?"'

They were just by the little grave now; and still Emily would not speak. However much they hurt her (and now one of them was pinching the skin under her armpit) she wouldn't say a word. Being so close to Emily Nott, scarcely two yards from where she lay, she was strong with the sense of their secret communion. No one must ever know, no grown-up person, ever, ever, ever. She bit her lip and tears tickled her face, and the bell in the church tower tolled a last toll which vibrated on the still hot air.

"Take you to your mother, see if she can get some sense out of you . . ."

And now the funeral party had gone into the church; so the Crocodile Women pulled Emily between them to the lych-gate and through it, and up the village street, and her mother was leaning over the garden-gate because she'd been watching the funeral. Her mother had seen her with the Crocodile Women, and now she began to run down the street towards them.

"Why did you steal them? Why?"

They went on at her, and soon her mother's voice was joined with theirs; but the questions were as meaningless to her as her answers, if she had spoken, would have been to them. She and they inhabited different worlds, and no language could cross the frontiers between them; they might as well have tried to talk to Emily Nott, under her soft tummock of mossy grass, as to wrest her secret from Emily Am.

# Sunfish

*As he chugged back from his lobster-pots Long Tom met*
the drifters coming out of harbour on the morning tide.
There were five of them, and if Long Tom hadn't been so
addicted to beer and idleness, perhaps there would have
been six. His own boat, the *Girl Betsy,* was rusting alongside the quay with broken-down engines; and as his wife
never failed to point out to him at least twice a day, the
money which should be spent on the repair of the engines
was spent on beer and the time which should be occupied
in making more money was wasted in idleness. His brother,
to whom he owed five pounds, frequently lectured him in
similar terms; but Long Tom, who was old and lazy and
profligate, took precious little notice of either of them and
pottered about contentedly catching lobsters and crabs, long-
lining for congers, and taking visitors for fishing-trips in the
bay. In this fashion he earned just enough money to keep
him in beer.

Now he happened to notice, as the drifters crossed his
bows, a flurry of herring-gulls dipping and wheeling a hundred yards beyond them, and being himself as inquisitive
as the gulls, he altered course to see what the fuss was about.
The manœuvre took him under the stern of the *Girl Jean,*
from which his brother, leaning over the side, demanded
when he was going to pay back the five pounds. Long
Tom caught the adjectives "lazy," "good-for-nothing" and
"drunken," but the wind blew away the rest; so he waved
cheerfully and held his course, thinking how dull it must
be to be as hard-working, upright and respectable as his
brother, who was a teetotaller and regularly went to chapel
and was said to have two thousand pounds tucked away
in the bank.

When he approached, the gulls flew away; and he saw
an object in the water which looked like a large dead fish.
Most men would have left it at that, for there is little profit
in dead fishes, however large; but not Long Tom, who
was a kind of sea-scavenger and who thought that he would
save himself the trouble of seeking farther for bait for his
lobster-pots. He therefore carried on until the object was
alongside his beam, when he perceived that it was indeed
a fish, though a most extraordinary one, and moreover
that it was alive. It was about the size of a beer-barrel (that
was the comparison which first came into Long Tom's mind)
but in shape it was somewhat globular. It was tailless and
it had no proper fins, but propelled itself along by means of
two flappers which worked exactly like a pair of sculls. Its
head was huge, with big, staring eyes and a remarkably small
pursed-up mouth, and it wore an expression similar to
that of a sucking-pig. Tom knew what it was, because he
had a long memory and his uncle, who had also been a
drunken old sea-scavenger, had brought one into the har-

bour forty years ago. It was a Sunfish, which comes up to
bask on the surface of the water only in the hottest summers.
But it was either sick or sleepy, or as lazy as Long Tom
himself, for it moved its flappers feebly and hardly troubled
to get out of the way of the boat. Even when Long Tom
leaned over the side and put the gaff into its fat shoulder it
did not struggle, but allowed itself to be pulled up to the
gunwale with no more protest than a weary flop. Perhaps,
thought Tom, it was drunk with sun like the half-naked
trippers who slumbered on the sands. One good heave, and
he had it safely in the boat where it lay gasping, and stared
at him reproachfully with goggling eyes.

Immediately Tom regretted that he had put the gaff
into it. If he could get it home alive perhaps he'd be able
to sell it to an aquarium, or even to the Zoo. So he began
to make a great fuss of his sea-monster, dragging it into the
shade of the seat and splashing it with sea-water to revive
it. Then he made for harbour as fast as he could; but
half-way there his engine stopped—it was a frequent accident in any boat owned by Tom—and he was compelled
to row while the poor monster's gasps became shorter and
the hot sun dried the moisture from its skin. Every few
minutes Tom stopped and dipped the baler in the sea and
sprinkled the fish as if it were an exhausted boxer before the
last round. "Cheer up, little pig," he said, to encourage it;
but the Sunfish only opened its tiny mouth the wider, an
expression of babyish petulance came into its puckered face,
and the brightness faded from its mournful eyes. At last
when Tom was within a few yards of the quayside a brief
tremor passed over its body and it died.

When he had tied up the launch Tom pulled it out from
under the seat, just to make sure it was really dead, and as
he was doing so he heard a child's squeaky voice say "Look,

Auntie, look what the man's got! What a funny fish!" He looked up, and there was a middle-aged lady whose goggle-eyes behind thick glasses were rather like the Sunfish's eyes, and a small girl with blue bows in her hair dancing with excitement on the quay wall. "Take care, missie, as you don't fall," said Long Tom, "and if you waits, I'll let you see the Monster of the Deep." He hooked the gaff once more into the fish's shoulder and carried it up the slippery steps; it weighed, he thought, about twenty pounds.

"What an extraordinary creature!" said the lady as he laid it on the ground. "Does it bite?"

"Bite?" said Tom, "Lor' bless you, lady, he could nip off a man's hand as easy as winking."

He regretted this remark as soon as he had made it, for the short-sighted lady leaned forward to examine the fish more closely, and observed after a pause:

"But surely it has a very small mouth, hasn't it?"

"Oh, that ain't its mouth, ma'am," said Tom swiftly, making the best of a bad job.

The lady's expression became prim, and she pursed her lips so that she looked more than ever like the Sunfish. "I beg your pardon," she said. "Er—come away, Priscilla." Then she fumbled in her purse and brought out sixpence. "Thank you, my man. . . . Come away, Priscilla, from the nasty dead fish." And she dragged off the protesting child by the arm.

As he put the sixpence in his pocket the light of a sudden revelation dawned upon Long Tom and he perceived that there was money in the Sunfish even though it was dead. He covered it up with a sheet of canvas and hurried home, where he filled a bucket with water and fetched a wheelbarrow out of his back yard. As he was wheeling it away his wife came out of the cottage and shrilled at him, asking

a lot of questions to which she immediately supplied her
own answers:

"Why are you home so early? Want to be on the doorstep
when the pubs open. How many lobsters did you catch?
None, I suppose, same as usual. What are you doing with
that wheelbarrow? Going to sell it, eh, to raise some money.
And what will you do with the money? Swig it down your
throat same as ever . . ." Tom knew very well that it was
useless to argue with her, so he observed mildly that he was
going off on business and hurried away. Her shrill mono-
logue of question and answer pursued him up the street.

"And what sort of business, may I ask? Hanging about
on the quay. And where else do you carry on your business?
In the Red Lion. And where else? In the Three Pilchards.
And where else? In the Lord Nelson. And what do you do
there? Gossip, gossip, gossip. And whose is that wheelbarrow,
anyhow? Mine, and I'll have the Law on you if you sell it . . ."

Tom waved to her unconcernedly, and smiled to himself
because she reminded him of the ventriloquist who performed all day in one of the beach-booths. He trundled
down the crooked narrow street to the sea-front, where he
passed the time of day with the man who hired the deck-
chairs and with the bathing-attendant man and the ice-cream
man and the car-park attendant, and was pleased to find
that the beach was crowded, for it was the Saturday morning
of a Bank Holiday week-end. There wasn't a cloud in the
sky, and it was going to be a real scorcher, said the ice-cream
man with a cheerful grin. And indeed, when Tom reached
the quayside and lifted the sheet off his Sunfish a humming
swarm of bluebottles rose up from it and he had to swill
it with water from his bucket to wash their yellow eggs
away. Then he laid it carefully in the wheelbarrow, with
the bucket ready so that he could moisten it from time to

time, and set off towards the beach; but before he got there
he had another idea, and collected an armful of seaweed
from the rocks, with which he decked and surrounded the
monster, making for it a fanciful nest of sea-lettuce and
bladder-wrack.

Now he was ready; and as he approached the many-
coloured crowd on the beach he began to cry in a loud
and tuneful voice (for Tom could sing beautifully and indeed did sing almost every night in the Red Lion, the Three
Pilchards and the Lord Nelson):

"Walk up, ladies and gentlemen, walk up and see the
Wonder of the Deep. Never bin caught for forty years, never
bin seen in any menargerie, zoo, or 'quarium, never bin kept
in captivity before, walk up and see the Monster all alive-o!"

A score of excited children were his first customers. They
appeared as if from nowhere, like the flies, as soon as he
stopped pushing the barrow. They duly admired the monster and prodded it timidly with their fingers, and asked
if it were really alive, whereupon Tom in a great voice
replied shamelessly:

"All alive-o, young ladies and gentlemen, but just at the
moment he's havin' his siesta. Sunfish he's called because
of his habit of sleeping in the sun. Walk up, everybody, and
see the Slumbering Sunfish!"

Some more children arrived. There was no profit in the
inquisitive brats, but they might, thought Tom, serve as a
bait for their parents. And sure enough before long a
woman in a green bathing-dress trotted up shouting, "Donald! Donald! What's my Donald up to!" and another woman
appeared calling breathlessly, "Margie, I won't have you
buying winkles from strange men!" and these were followed
by a young man in trunks and a fat man with a towel round
his middle and a whiskered man whose chest and shoulders

were skinned by the sun so that he looked like a boiled lobster.

"Tuppence to see the Monster!" shouted Tom hopefully. "Tuppence to see the Wonder of the Deep all alive-o!" His audience, however, having no pockets in their bathing-dresses, made a perfunctory gesture of fumbling where their pockets should have been and walked away. Only one of the women, who carried a purse and was relieved to find that Margie had eaten no winkles, threw two pennies into the barrow, where they disappeared amongst the seaweed. This gave Tom a little encouragement, but he realised that he must change his tactics so he wheeled the barrow off the beach on to the sea-front, where the majority of people were at least partly dressed in the kind of clothes which had pockets. Here he borrowed from the ice-cream man a card-board box and cut a slit in its lid. "Lend us a few pennies," he said to the ice-cream man. "For bait." The ice-cream man good-humouredly put in fourpence, so that Tom was able to rattle the box while he shouted:

"Now then, ladies and gentlemen, walk up to see the Sunfish what tore my nets to pieces with its savage jaws! Five pounds' worth of damage it done to my nets, and I can't go fishing again till I gets 'em mended! Come and see the savage Sunfish what can snap through a steel hawser as if it was ice-cream!"

These new tactics proved much more successful; soon the cardboard box became quite heavy and Tom was gratified to see a few sixpences go in with the coppers. But it was thirsty work, and at noon, accompanied by a loud hum of bluebottles, he pushed his barrow to the Red Lion, covered it with the sheet and went inside to count his takings. They amounted to six and sevenpence halfpenny, so he was able to remain in the Red Lion until a quarter past two, when

he borrowed from the landlord the handbell which was
being employed to draw his attention to the fact that it
was past closing time.

There were three cats, one black, one ginger and one
tortoiseshell, sitting round his wheelbarrow when he came
out of the pub. He drove them away by ringing the bell,
and he continued to ring it all the way to the sea-front.
In this fashion he attracted a horde of children, who followed
him as if he were the Pied Piper and formed the nucleus
of the crowd which gathered as soon as he set his barrow
down next door to the ice-cream man. The beer he had
drunk gave strength to his voice and wings to his imagination. "Never bin caught for fifty years!" he hollered. "Never
will be caught for another fifty! Walk up to see the flying
fish what can't fly! Half an animal, half a fish, and half a
bird! Cross between a pig and a basking shark and don't
ask me how it happened! Come and see the Basking Sunfish,
straight from the tropics, threepence a look, never bin
caught for seventy-five years, and don't forget the Beer
Drinker's Benevolent Fund!" He rattled the box, which
was rapidly filling with coppers. "Don't touch him, lady or
he'll wake up, and he's terrible savage! Mind the little girl's
fingers, Missus; I wouldn't like for her to lose them. Dragged
him up fifty fathoms I did, and he tore my nets to ribbons
with his horrid jaws. Walk up and see the Man-eating Sunfish!"

All through the blazing afternoon Long Tom rang his
bell and rattled his box and hollered so loud that the com-
motion even attracted the bathers from the beach and drew
from the foaming fringe of the sea the white bodies of the
new visitors and the brown bodies of the old visitors and
the pink parboiled bodies of the people who'd arrived the
day before yesterday. Long Tom only paused for breath

when his box was full; and then he hurried across to the
ice-cream man who gladly changed his cargo of coppers
into silver and ten-shilling notes, for the ice-cream man was
also doing a roaring trade.

Towards six o'clock, however, the crowd on the seafront
became thinner, and Tom decided to knock off for the day.
He visited the Red Lion, the Three Pilchards and the Lord
Nelson in that order; and as he wheeled his barrow from
pub to pub he was followed by the black cat, the ginger cat
and the tortoiseshell cat, and these were joined, as dusk fell,
by an indeterminate number of shyer and shadowy cats
which crept out of alleys and jumped down from window-
sills and slunk round street corners sniffing the air to windward of the barrow.

What was already apparent to their sharper noses attracted the attention next morning even of Long Tom's
anæsthetised nose. It forced itself still more insistently upon
the attention of his wife who neither drank nor smoked nor
took snuff; and as he was washing the Sunfish with salt-and-
water over the kitchen sink she suddenly flew at him with
abuse and rhetorical questions so shrill that they drove him
out of the house.

"What's the master of the *Girl Betsy* doing now? Muck-
ing about with a stinking fish in the kitchen. Why don't
he catch anything that folks can eat? Because he's too lazy.
What's happened to his brains, if he ever had any? Gone
rusty same as his boat's engines. What do his fine pals in
the pub say about him as soon as his back's turned? Soft
and silly. How did he spend the whole of yesterday, when
he ought to have bin at sea? Making a fool of himself before the visitors . . ."

Tom uttered no protest against these accusations. If he
had attempted to answer them he might have let out the

secret that he had nine pounds in notes stuffed into his
waistcoat pocket, which was more money than he had
possessed for years. So he humped the Sunfish on his shoulder and went out, followed by curses and flies.

He laid the monster tenderly in the wheelbarrow, and
rearranged its nest of seaweed, and even placed a few sun-
flower heads from the garden, symbolic of its name and
nature, in a circular pattern round it. All the same, he was
unable to conceal from himself the fact that its pristine
splendour had fled. It shone no longer in the barrow like
a great globule of silver, but was become flaccid and grey.
Its sad eyes, glazed over with a pale film, had a watery look,
and the expression on its face was utterly woebegone. Long
Tom, who had become curiously fond of his Sunfish, was
saddened by its approaching dissolution. Yesterday it had
seemed so fantastical, so weird, so altogether improbable, a
Wonder of the Deep indeed; to-day, it was just another
dead fish with an extremely powerful smell. Tom shrugged
his shoulders and made his way thoughtfully to the sea-front.

It was another blue day, the beach was already swarming
with visitors, and in spite of the unpleasing appearance of
the Sunfish Tom had a profitable morning. He made up
for the deficiencies of his monster by an improving tech-
nique, for he sang its praises in ever more extravagant terms,
and sometimes, even, there leapt unbidden to his lips a sort
of wild poetry that came he knew not whence as he described
the dim green weedy grottoes of the deep-sea-bottom which
he had never seen. All the morning without intermission he
bore witness to the glories of the Sunfish while the Sunfish
rotted before his eyes. It was as if he sought to stay with
words the inevitable consequences of mortality, as poets have
done before now with as little success as Tom had. And so
like an evangelist he preached to the white bodies and the

brown bodies and the pink bodies and to the bodies which glistened, themselves like sea-monsters, with anti-sunburn oil.

About noon he happened to pass close to the ventriloquist's booth and borrowed from that indefatigable person an illusory trick or two which worked, for a short time, very well. He plunged his hands into the seaweed and thus contrived to animate the Sunfish, raising up its head for a moment and allowing it to fall back into the slippery barrow with a wriggling flop while he shouted, "All alive-o!" In this fashion he deceived an earnest old lady, who protested that it was cruel to keep the poor thing out of water in the hot sun. A moment later, however, she moved round to windward of the barrow, and protested no more.

Alas, by mid-afternoon it became impossible to play this trick any longer. It was no use Tom asserting that the Sunfish was alive-o, since the monster itself with nauseous insistence contradicted him, and the very flies rose up with an indignant hum to declare him a liar. The crowd round his barrow began to melt away, and even the ice-cream man protested that Tom was ruining his trade. So he wheeled the barrow on to the beach in search of fresh custom, on to the beach which by now was so crowded that it looked from the sea-front like a garden filled with flowers or a rich carpet of a thousand hues cunningly intermingled. But wherever Tom went, a little hole or tear appeared suddenly in the carpet through which the fascinated ice-cream man could see the brown sand.

The sunbathers sniffed and muttered, and pulled the newspapers off their faces, and hurriedly moved away; others picked up their deck-chairs and carried them up-wind of Tom; embracing couples broke off their amorous games and fled from him; even the children abandoned their half-

finished sand-castles to the tide. What few pennies found
their way into Tom's box now came from windward; and
when the breeze died down towards evening nobody ventured near enough to put in any pennies at all.

However, it hadn't been a bad day; and when Tom took
himself off to the Red Lion he was the richer by seven
pounds three and tuppence, and he was able for the first
time since the *Girl Betsy's* engines broke down to buy
drinks all round. He made the same grandiose gesture in the
Three Pilchards and the Lord Nelson; and by then he was
too merry to notice that the people who drank his health
and wished him jolly good luck did so from a respectful
distance. For wherever he went now, an aura of the Sunfish
hung about him; and even the fat cheerful barmaid of the
Lord Nelson, who often declared that she had a soft spot in
her heart for the old rogue, sheered away from him when
he leaned over the bar.

By closing time he was very drunk indeed, and he sang
his way happily down the crooked street, through the alley,
and along the water-side. The drifters were back from their
fishing, and the fish quay was slippery with fins and skins
and entrails and slime. Suddenly Long Tom's unsteady feet
skidded from under him and down he went; the barrow
turned over and the Sunfish fell out with a dull plop. Tom
knocked the back of his head on the ground, and as he was
picking himself up bewilderedly a familiar voice greeted
him with the words "good-for-nothing," "lazy," and "drunk
again." It was his brother, respectable, sober and industrious
as usual, who had only just finished swabbing down the decks
of the *Girl Jean.*

"Same old story," said his brother. "Wasting your time
in the pubs while the rest of us go fishing. And what about
that five pounds you owe me?"

He was even more ill-tempered than usual, because he'd had a poor catch of skates and dogfish and a shark had torn his nets to pieces when he was catching pilchards for bait. "What about that five pounds?" he repeated, but only as a matter of form, for he had long ago given up hope that Tom would pay him back. Indeed, he used the phrase nowadays as a sort of conventional greeting to his brother, instead of saying "Good morning" or "Good night." So he hastened away without waiting for an answer, and he never knew that Tom was at that moment fumbling in his waistcoat-pocket full of pound notes.

The sound of his steady and respectable steps, teetotaller's, chapelgoer's steps, died away in the distance, and Tom was alone on the darkening quayside. The Sunfish lay at his feet, and the night was kind to it, for the signs of corruption were no longer visible and a faint mystical luminosity glorified its last hours. Oblivious of its smell, Tom leaned down to wonder at its extraordinary shape, its curious oar-like fins, its lack of a tail, its little pig-like face and its pursed-up mouth no larger in diameter than a man's finger. How did it eat and what did it eat, how in Heaven's name did it capture its prey in those dim, faraway deeps where it had its being? Tom did not know; but he felt a sudden surge of joy and astonishment at the multiplicity and strangeness of all living things that flooded his heart like the surge of the tide now racing up the river. He turned his head, and looked out to sea, and allowed his wandering thoughts to people it with even stranger monsters than the Sunfish— the sea-horse and the sea-serpent, the octopus and the whale, and that Leviathan which played therein; yes, and with a myriad creatures more fantastical still, creatures of every shape and size and hue, unnamed, unseen, unimagined, unbelievable, never bin caught for a hundred years, never bin caught before. Who knows, thought Tom, that some of them may not be riding in on this very tide, who knows what to-morrow's tide and the next day's may not bring up out of the vasty deep? And at this thought a huge happiness filled him, and as he picked up the Sunfish and laid it once more in his wheelbarrow he began to sing in a loud and drunken voice the praises of his Creator:

"All things wise and wonderful!"

sang Tom, as he slithered and staggered along the slimy quay. Before him went the Sunfish like an immense glow-worm, making a pool of green light in the bottom of the wheelbarrow. Behind him followed seven cats with questing noses and tails in the air.

# A Cold Wind Blowing

*The weather was cold for April, and the north-easter* which rattled the windows of the old Rectory bore a flurry of late snow. But it was a warm and pungent smell, it was like a faint whiff of the Indian Ocean, of the fabulous islands of spice, which greeted the Canon when he entered the breakfast-room, as they still called it—though nowadays they had lunch and tea there too, and the supper which they indomitably described as dinner, and the Canon's wife knitted and made her rag rugs there, and he smoked and dozed and dreamt and at the desk in the corner wrote his sermons and his never-to-be-finished book on the Life and Theology of Saint Thomas Aquinas.

"Ah!" said the Canon, and sniffed. "So you didn't forget," he added.

"I never have, have I?" And indeed in forty-five years she had never once forgotten. It wasn't the kind of thing you *could* forget, if you were the wife of a clergyman. But she smiled, glad of his appreciation, and they sat down to breakfast.

"You'll have your cereal first?"

"I think——" He hesitated. "Yes, I think I'll start with *them*, straight away. Greedy of me, perhaps: like missing out the bread-and-butter at a children's party!"

Food meant a lot to them now they were growing old, now that the Canon no longer had his golf, nor she her bridge, except on the rare occasions when some old friends dropped in; for they had sold their little car two or three Budgets ago. Sometimes the Canon, who had never been a self-indulgent man, became quite alarmed at the way meals loomed large in his thoughts, and breathed absurd little apologies to God about it. After all, it wasn't very nice to start thinking about a boiling-fowl three days before you ate it, even if you could only afford a boiling-fowl once in six weeks. He'd been thinking about these hot-cross buns all the time he was shaving.

"Tommy Briggs brought them round," said his wife as she poured out the coffee.

The Canon shook his head gravely. It seemed only yesterday that he'd had the painful duty of sacking Tommy Briggs from the choir, for "talking smut" and swearing; he'd heard him say, "Damn your eyes," to another boy, actually *inside* the church. Then Tommy had left school and become the baker's roundsman, which gave him all sorts of opportunities for idling and gossiping and mischief at people's back doors. One day the Canon's wife had caught him, red-handed as she oddly described it, kissing the little maid who came in three days a week to clean up. She had subsequently dismissed the little maid; and had not been quite sure whether she did so because of the outrage in the kitchen or because of the pressing need to save money now that the prices of

everything went up and up and up. Certainly she believed
that kissing was something not quite nice in itself—and
there had been more to it than kissing: the girl had been
pressed hard against the kitchen dresser, Tommy's body to
hers! It was not the sort of spectacle one could comfortably
describe to the Canon; so she had just told him, "I caught
them kissing and I told Jean she could take her notice, as
soon as he had gone." Later the Canon had seen Tommy
and given him a good talking to, about Purity in Word
and Deed.

"I fear that there are bad influences in that boy's house,"
he pronounced, stirring the sugar into his coffee. "His father
is *very Left,* I am told."

"He shouldn't be, he's got a good job," said the Canon's
wife. "They tell me men get twelve pounds a week at the
factory, and if they work on Saturday it's overtime." Twelve
pounds a week. Perhaps thirteen. That was six hundred and
fifty a year, and the Canon got four hundred plus his Easter
Offering, which was taxed as if it were income! So often
nowadays they found themselves comparing their income
with the wages of the working-classes, or with what they
thought the village grocer earned, or with what a village
girl could get as a typist, almost as soon as she left school.
It was only of late that this envy had crept into their lives
—an unwelcome stranger, for it was in neither of their
natures to be envious. They struggled against the evil thing,
and the Canon made it a subject of his private prayers. Again
and again they would remind each other: We mustn't grumble, we've had a good life, we've got a roof over our heads,
we've got each other. Yet always it came back, the blind
resentment against a changing world; and the reminder that
they'd once kept a gardener, and two maids who only had
one afternoon out and were always in by nine-thirty—that

they used to give quite big Rectory tennis-parties and that they always spent their holidays at Aix-les-Bains—this didn't really comfort them; it deepened the pitiful, puzzled resentment which vaguely expressed itself in the words *It isn't fair*. It wasn't fair, it didn't make sense, that a man who simply put together aeroplane-engines should earn more than a Canon who was also an M.A. Cantab. and a Doctor of Divinity.

"Besides, they don't have to try to keep up appearances, as we do," the Canon's wife went on. "Goodness knows when *you* last had a new suit; or a new shirt, for that matter."

"I *like* old clothes." He smiled. "But you, my dear—"

"Oh, it doesn't matter, we never go anywhere."

"I know, it's dull for you. I've got my work."

"I'm not complaining. But the bills worry me. We never *used* to have bills, and let them go on. Why, they've even got a TV."

"Who has?"

"The Briggs. On the hire-purchase, I daresay. But with his twelve pounds a week, and now Tommy's working in the bakery another six or seven as well, I suppose they can afford it."

"But we don't want a TV, do we?" the Canon said.

"No . . . but it would be nice, now we're old, to sit and watch it in the evenings."

"Ah well, we mustn't grumble." He added, with only the faintest shade of irony, "We must be content in that station into which it has pleased God to call us. Now let us sample Tommy's hot-cross buns."

"I'll go and fetch them. I always heat them up a bit, under the gas-grill."

She went out, and he sat and listened to the rattle of the window-frames. There always seemed to be a wind blowing about the Rectory nowadays; and goodness! it was the twenty-second of April, yet there were snowflakes melting on the pane. His old mind went back to other springs, long ago, blue days with pollen-smudged bees buzzing in the crocuses, when surely there had never been a cold wind blowing. Daffodils in the borders, and even a few tulips, by the twenty-second of April, and old Wilkins marking out the tennis-court . . .

His wife came back with the big covered plate which used to hold the buttered tea-cakes, in their palmy days. The smell from the Spice Islands, Java and Sumatra came with her. He made the observation which he'd made almost unconsciously, once a year for two-score of years:

"I can't help wishing, somehow, that they'd sell them without the—er—Symbol. If you think about it, it's not quite—*decent*, is it?"

He'd always eaten them, all the same. He added now:

"—or if we could have them on other days, not this special one."

"Then they wouldn't be a treat," she said briskly, hardly comprehending what was in his mind.

"I suppose not. But in these hard times, it's nice to have something *different*."

"Yes."

She took the lid off the tea-cake dish and put two buns on his plate.

"Now don't worry about the butter this morning. Have plenty. It's a treat."

But he noticed that she only took the merest sliver of butter herself. She was always like that. He said to himself, fondly foolish: She's a bit of a saint, really; and promptly apologized to God for the extravagance.

"Oh dear . . . ," she was saying.

"Yes? Yes? What's the matter?"

"But *look*."

She was staring at her plate, and now he looked down at his. At first he could not see anything wrong with the buns. They were brown and shiny, with quite a lot of currants showing. And then at last he understood.

"The Cross . . ."

That was the point. It wasn't a cross; it wasn't even the rough indentation which passes for a cross. Drawn in the soft dough with a careful forefinger, upon every bun, was a Hammer and Sickle.

"That Tommy Briggs . . . It's monstrous, wicked; it's *blasphemous . . .*," the Canon's wife was saying.

The Canon sat and stared at the two ridiculous buns, and the wind got up outside, and he listened to it and thought again of the tranquil springs of his yesteryears. He was suddenly aware of all the winds of the world blowing about him, and he didn't understand them; there had never been such winds before. He half heard his wife say: "But we couldn't eat them, could we, after that?" and he nodded. She added, in a queer, flat voice that sounded both puzzled and afraid:

"I'll go and fetch your cereal."

She went into the kitchen and he sat still, listening to the wind.

# Tiger, Tiger

*The birth of Emilio was a great embarrassment to his* mother, whose husband had been absent for three years with the army in Morocco and was shortly expected home on leave; so as soon as the child was weaned she sold him to the gypsy-woman who begged at the corner of the Calle Larios. The gitana wrapped him in dirty rags and squeezed upon his face and arms some juice from the stem of a wild yellow poppy called *Chelidonium*. This raised large blisters which gave him a pitiable appearance though they did him no permanent harm. The gitana then took up her accustomed station at the street corner bearing the blistered baby in her arms. Whenever a prosperous-looking passer-by came near she tweaked the baby's bottom, which made him howl; she then held him out under the very nose of the passer-by and chanted in her professional whining voice, "See, señor, the *niño* cries because he is hungry."

The child's horrible tetters, the stink of his wrappings,

and his loud cries excited such compassion that the gypsy's
takings were doubled; moreover, her victims were so frightened of infection—for the blisters simulated smallpox—
that they never waited long enough to search through their
pockets for the very smallest coin. She prospered greatly; and
apart from the pinchings and blisterings she treated the
child with kindness, and even with a sort of affection, croon-
ing him to sleep every night with the old monotonous gypsy
songs. Indeed he thrived so well in her care that he
soon became too heavy for her withered arms to hold, and
she was compelled to buy another baby. Thereafter, when
she went begging, Emilio was left at home; and in her smelly
hovel he crawled, toddled, played, had whooping-cough,
mumps and measles, and acquired some useful immunities
against the diseases which more pampered brats frequently
die of. As his world grew wider he continued his education
in the yard at the rear of the hovel, where he picked up
from the neighbors some startling swear-words, played at
bull-fights with a mongrel puppy, and discovered a God.

The object of his worship was an old, broken-down, pelota-
player called José, dying of drink and other excesses, whose
cottage abutted on the bottom end of the yard. This José
possessed a chair with a broken leg, which he shored up
with a packing-case and upon which he sat for most of the
day, slumbering, dreaming and remembering in the sun.
From time to time, when his memories crowded most insistently upon him, he would take the boy Emilio upon his
knee and tell him wondrous tales. Tigers, elephants, cobras
and pythons peopled these stories, for in his youth a strange
chance had taken the pelota-player into the Malayan
jungle. A promoter of the game had paid his fare to Shang-
hai, where pelota was exceedingly popular; and there José

had met a visiting Rajah who on a sudden whim had employed him to introduce it into his kingdom.

The Rajah, who did nothing by halves, built a pelota-court two hundred and fifty yards long in the grounds of his palace and rewarded with gold and dancing girls the young men who showed the greatest aptitude under José's tuition. Never, surely, had pelota been played in circumstances of such pomp and splendour! The Rajah watched it from a gilded box hung with the rarest tapestries; in another box, only slightly less gorgeous, the Rajah's fifteen wives giggled and applauded behind their veils; a score of musicians played upon silver instruments an air which had been specially composed to match the urgent rhythm of the game; and a silver-voiced eunuch of the Rajah's household, who had been trained to act as *cantara,* chanted the score from a vantage-point on the back of an elephant whose tusks were tipped with beaten gold.

"Very strange it was," mused José, as he looked back upon this scene through a heat-haze of years and wine, "to close your eyes and listen to the thud of the ball just as you might hear it in Madrid or Bilbao; and then suddenly to open your eyes and see the elephant standing there, and the monkeys and the long-tailed parakeets watching the game from the tops of the tall jungle trees . . ."

It was at this point in the story that Emilio generally interrupted:

"Tell me about the jungle, José! Tell me about the tigers!"

"Ah, the jungle . . ." and José would gravely nod his head, for of all tropical phenomena the terror of the jungle, and the ferocity of its teeming population, had impressed itself upon him most powerfully. He had once been lost, for a few hours, in the green wilderness which lay all around the Rajah's palace; and the horror of this experience had never left him. "A fearful place is the jungle, my little one," —and then he would describe the emerald twilight beneath the trees and the hot green smell of it, the swishings in the long grass and the chitter-chatter in the tree-tops, and all the sounds which never cease by night or day, whistlings, wailings, chirrupings, screechings, purrings, howlings, brayings, roarings.

He would describe, too, the various beasts which made these sounds, and draw them with the point of his stick in the dust at his feet: "Those are tigers. See their striped sides. See their terrible claws." Very savage they looked as he pictured them, rampant, snarling, pouncing, charging— "For you must know, little one, that all these beasts are perpetually at war. It is a war with a million casualties every day which had no beginning and will never have an end. Oh, I have shuddered to listen to it as I lay awake under my mosquito-net! First you hear a hungry howl, like this ——" And Emilio's eyes grew wide with delicious terror as old José imitated the devilish shriek of a hyena. "And then perhaps the whole jungle echoes to a mighty roar"—he roared so loud that Emilio nearly jumped out of his skin —"and next comes the dreadful silence when every living creature waits, and waits, and waits, for the squeal which dies almost before it is born. Then all the jungle-noises suddenly break loose again as if the beasts are glad that the waiting is over, the birds flap squawking from the trees, monkeys chatter, elephants trumpet, hyenas bray, everywhere the feet go pitter-pat, and above all these noises the tiger roars, once, twice, three times, to tell the jungle he has made his kill. At last all the other noises die away, and you hear this one, which is the worst of the lot. Listen!"

Emilio would lay his head against José's body so that he could listen to the tiger purring in his belly, a wonderful rumbling purr, like a cat's only louder, and so full of awful contentment that you could almost hear in it the tearing of flesh and the crunching of bones!

"Like that, little one, is the jungle," summed up José when he could purr no longer, "where the strong have slain the weak, and the swift have leapt upon the slow, and the hale have got fat upon the crippled, ever since God made it millions and millions of years ago . . . And now jump off my knee, for I've roared and purred till I'm thirsty and I'm going round to the café to drink a bottle of wine."

One day when Emilio was nearly six José fell sick and could no longer hobble out of his cottage to sit in the sun on the chair with the broken leg. Emilio heard him groaning within the cottage, but the sound frightened him and he did not go near. All day he drew striped tigers in the dust, and the wind blew away these tigers, which were as unsubstantial as dreams. Towards evening José began calling for him, and he crept timidly to the broken window and peered through it at the old man tossing on his truckle-bed. "It is in my back," moaned José, raising himself upon his elbows, "and it is surely a foretaste of the torments of hell. There is only one thing which might cure it, and that is a bottle of wine; but alas, I cannot walk as far as the wineshop to fetch one. Are *you* brave enough, little one, to go to Baldomero's wine-shop down by the harbour and fetch me a bottle of his second-best rioja? Otherwise I shall assuredly die."

Now Emilio had never ventured alone more than a few paces away from the door of the hovel, because the gypsy had threatened to flay the hide off him if he played in the

street. He had been quite content with his little world of
the back yard. The prospect of the punishment which he
would receive from the gypsy frightened him very much.
On the other hand, it was unthinkable that his God should
be allowed to perish for the want of a bottle of wine. He
hesitated, and José said wheedlingly:

"First, I will tell you a tale about the jungle; but you
must promise that when the tale is done you will fetch me
the wine."

"Tell me then," said Emilio, "the story about when you
were lost"—for that was the most exciting tale of all.

José groaned. "It is a very long one, and I doubt if I
shall live to finish it," he said, "but this is how it begins.
As I was returning from a hunt one day the twilight fell
suddenly, and in the darkness I took the wrong path. I was a
young man then, and I was not, I think, lacking in courage;
indeed, I had actually toyed with the idea of becoming a
matador before I took up pelota instead. The bull-ring held
no terrors for me. Yet I tell you, Emilio, that although fifty
years have passed since that night, I still wake up in a cold
sweat of fear at the memory of the perils that beset me in
that hour!"

Then, between groanings and wheezings, José decribed
those perils one by one—cobras whose bite would prove
fatal in less than three minutes, hamadryads twelve feet
long which could spit their venom like poisoned arrows
(asserted José) and slay their victims from afar, pythons
coiled in the trees, indistinguishable from the green boughs,
whose squeeze would break every bone in a man's body.

"So much for the snakes," groaned José, "but the snakes
are nothing compared with the four-footed beasts." Then
he told of the ferocious water-buffalo which charged like an
express train, of the rhinoceros which trampled its enemies
to scarlet pulp ("like jam, Emilio, like jam"), of the rogue

elephant which threw its victims over the tallest tree. "But even these," said José, "are not to be feared so much as the great cats, because at least you can hear them coming."

He went on to speak of the leopard which made no footfall, the black panther as swift as the wind, and the terrible tiger which, he declared, with a mere playful cuff of its paw could strike off a man's head. "Picture me, then, alone among all these hazards in the dark forest. I tried one path, and lo! it led me to the bank of a wide river which was full, it seemed, of teak-logs floated down by the lumbermen; yet even as I paused on the bank all the logs opened their mouths wide and I perceived that they were alligators. I turned and fled back the way I had come; and as I ran I could hear stealthy beasts padding behind me on their terrible, quiet feet. The moon rose over the tree-tops, and suddenly I saw its light reflected in a hundred eyes——"

"Yes, yes, tell me about the eyes!" cried Emilio, who had heard this story a great many times before and never grew tired of it.

"Eyes all round me," José went on, "some green, some amber, some pale as the moon; and some as red as the Rajah's rubies—or as blood. They peered at me out of the trees and out of the undergrowth and out of the tall grass; I swear there were half a hundred eyes watching me as I went in terror down the path!"

At this point José interrupted his story, and groaned pitiably indeed.

"The very thought of it makes me sweat," he said, "and the pain in my back grows worse, and my mouth is so parched that I can scarcely speak. Unless I have something to drink very quickly, it is quite certain that I shall die. Run, run, for the love of God, to Baldomero's wine-shop at the end of the quay!"

At the sight of poor José writhing in agony, tears started

in Emilio's eyes, and he forgot all about his fear of the un-
known streets and the gypsy's threat to beat the hide off him.
He would have braved a whole jungleful of tigers for the
sake of his God! He jumped down off the window-sill, and
José said:

"There's a brave fellow! But not so fast; first I must give
you some money, and tell you the way. Come round by
the back door." So Emilio entered the cottage which smelt
of stale drink and bad drains, and José with many heart-
breaking groans sought through his pockets for pesetas. He
pressed these into Emilio's small hand which had never held
any money before, and Emilio gripped them tight.

"You go straight down the street," said José, "until you
come to a promenade with bright lights, and that is called
the Paseo de la Alameda. You count the turnings as you
pass along it, and you go down the third one, which is
called the Street of the Fourteenth of April. At the end of
that street you see the ships in the harbour just in front of
you, and on the corner, at the very end of the street, is
Baldomero's wine-shop. You cannot possibly miss it. Give
Baldomero the pesetas, and say you want a bottle of the
second-best rioja for poor old José the pelota-player who
is dying with pains in his back. But hurry, for the love of
Mary, hurry, or perhaps I shall be dead before you return!"

The first part of the journey was surprisingly easy,
although it was already getting dark when Emilio set out.
He ran down to the end of the street, and sure enough he
emerged into a noisy world of bright lights, full of rattling
trams and hurrying people. The trams disconcerted him at
first, though he had seen them once before, when the gypsy
took him to pray in the great Cathedral at Christmas-time.
He soon grew accustomed to them, however, and he enjoyed

the feeling of independence and adventure as he strode
along the Paseo clutching the hot sticky coins in his fist. He
glanced at his reflection in the windows of the shops and
thought he looked very grown-up indeed; and the shops
themselves, with their many-coloured merchandise, excited
him so much that he almost forgot to count the turnings
as José had told him to do. The side street which he went
down at last was a very crooked and narrow one, and he
chose it rather doubtfully, believing it to be the third but
wondering at the same time whether it might not be the
second or the fourth. It was paved with cobble-stones, which
hurt his bare feet, and the houses on each side of the street
seemed to lean together, shutting out the sky. For the first
time he felt afraid, and he ran as fast as he could until at
last he came out into the open, and the harbour lay before
him, full of ships' masts like a little forest and riding-lights
swinging to and fro with the tide.

But there was no wine-shop on the corner, nor indeed
any shop at all, and with this discovery a sudden feeling of
helplessness descended upon Emilio. He felt as an astron-
omer might feel if his telescope sought in vain for some
predicted star: the ordered world dissolved into chaos. He
ran round and round in panic like a lost dog, and then,
growing afraid of the dark, he made blindly for the lights
of the quayside where he almost fell over a boy not very
much older than himself who sat cross-legged on the pavement before a piece of red felt and cried out to the passing
sailors how cheaply and beautifully he would polish their
shoes:

"Look out," said the *muchacho*, "or you'll knock my box
over, you clumsy little fool!"

Emilio humbly begged his pardon. "Please," he added
breathlessly, "will you tell me the way to Baldomero's wine-

shop at the corner of the Street of the Fourteenth of April?"

The *muchacho* looked up at him and grinned, showing very white teeth in a brown face. He had crinkly hair and those almond eyes which the Moors left behind them when they reeled back from Spain.

"In the name of God," he said, "what do you want with a wine-shop, small one?"

Emilio explained about José's illness and the old man's urgent need of a bottle of the second-best rioja lest he should certainly die; and he proudly displayed the pesetas which José had given him.

"Well, it's not far to the wine-shop," said the boot-black. "It's on the next corner, and you can't miss it because there's an old woman selling lottery-tickets outside. But you're so small that I'm sure Baldomero won't sell *you* any wine. He'll box your ears for asking!" The boot-black now stood up and he had very long spindly legs; he was head-and-shoulders taller than Emilio. "I'll tell you what I'll do," he grinned. "Seeing you're so small, *I'll* fetch the wine for you. Just give me the money, and stand and wait."

Emilio thanked him politely, while the boy folded his piece of red felt and picked up his box of brushes. "Just you wait here," he said, "and I'll be back in no time." But as soon as Emilio handed him the money, he spat out a rude word under his breath, laughed unpleasantly, said "Catch me if you can!" and ran away down the street on his spindly shanks. Emilio began to chase him, but his little legs were no match for those lanky ones; and the boot-black had plenty of time to turn round and make a long nose at him before he disappeared out of sight.

Emilio was still running, bewilderedly and without hope, when he collided with the legs of a man who was standing at the edge of the pavement.

"Kindly look where you're going," said the man. "I happen to be blind."

"Oh, I'm sorry!" said Emilio, who was strangely frightened of the blind man's soft and ingratiating voice and still more frightened of his soft hands which fondled his forehead.

"And who might this be?" went on the man, talking, it seemed, to himself. "Ah, a little boy, I see. Why do I say 'I see'? I do not see. But I *feel* long pointed ears, sticking out like a rabbit's. A small nose. A puckered-up face, I think, like an ugly little monkey's. I feel wet tears. What might be the matter?"

"Oh, please. I was looking for Baldomero's wine-shop."

"There it is. *There.* Bless me, you have eyes, yet you cannot see a wine-shop! I have no eyes, but I have stood here begging for twenty years and I can tell you exactly what you can see. You can see," said the blind man, in a terrible soft whisper, "a brightly-lit window, and inside the lights are shining on rows of bottles. Beauti-ful bottles, all full of beauti-ful wine! A man could even forget his blindness if he drank all that wine! And you can see some people leaning on a counter, and some people sitting at little tables, and a fat sweaty man in his shirt-sleeves pouring out the wine into glasses, for those that can afford to pay. Ha-ha! *For those that can afford to pay.* If you want wine, therefore, small rabbit with the wet face, go in and offer your pesetas and take what you will. And forget all about the poor old blind beggar standing in the cold outside."

"I have no pesetas," said Emilio. "A shoe-black stole them from me and ran away."

"Very well." The blind man spoke sharply now, and although his voice was still so quiet there was a sort of grating edge to it. "Very well. Then you can stand and look into the window of the wine-shop. You can watch the people drinking inside. Really, I think you are very fortunate indeed. I cannot even *watch* the people drinking."

He broke off suddenly to whine to a passer-by:

"Spare a coin for a poor old blind man!"

But the passer-by ignored him, and went on to the street-corner where he bought a lottery-ticket from the old woman who stood there calling *"Loteria Loteria!"* in a hoarse voice like that of some wild and lonely marsh-bird. The blind man resumed his strange, whispered conversation with himself, while the tips of his fingers still rested lightly on the top of Emilio's head; and somehow their light touch seemed to hold the boy to him, despite his fear and his desire to run away.

"It is a curious reflection," whispered the blind man, "that if one bought a winning ticket in the lottery—always supposing, of course, that one had the money to pay for it —one could buy up, not only Baldomero's wine-shop and all that's in it, but also the whole of the Street of the Fourteenth of April with all the houses and their contents."

*"Loteria,"* wailed the old woman. "Buy a lucky ticket in the *loteria!"*

"A curious reflection which always strikes me very forcibly on cold, wet nights. One could buy up, for example, the pawnbroker's which stands on the left of the wine-shop, with all that's in it: jewels, fine gowns, fur coats, and even my own poor fiddle with which I once earned my living and which I was compelled to part with for the price of a few drinks. . . . It occurs to me also that one could buy up the house which stands on the right of the pawnshop, which is much frequented by sailors and contains three good-looking girls. I speak from hearsay, mind you; I haven't seen them myself. But I understand they would give one a very warm welcome if one were the fortunate purchaser of a winning ticket in the lottery. Always supposing, ha-ha, that one had enough money to buy a ticket in the first place. . . . But you, small rabbit with the big ears? You are still crying. What are you crying for? The woes of the world?"

Suddenly the blind man's whisper rose to an angry screech.

"Bah! You are young, you have eyes. What have you got to cry about? Bah, go away, I am tired of you. Go away, you wet-nosed snivelling rabbit! Take *that!*"—and the soft hand that a moment before had been caressing the top of Emilio's head clawed across his face, tearing with crooked fingers at his eyes. The force of the blow sent him staggering across the pavement, where he crouched in terror against the door of the house next to the wine-shop. The blood from five long scratches mingled with his tears.

*"Loteria! Loteria!"* cried the old woman every few seconds, and the plaintive chant, like the wailing of the sea-gulls in the harbour, beat its way into Emilio's brain and echoed there like a requiem for his lost pesetas. Sobbing, he leaned in the doorway and let the world go by. At intervals, chilling his blood, he heard his tormentor whimpering, "Spare a coin for a poor old blind man." A man with a basket on his head marched to and fro calling "Fish heads and tails!" and a woman shrilly competed with him: "Flowers! Flowers! Roses and lilies! Buy your lady a bunch of flowers!" Once he heard—or perhaps he imagined it—his aunt's voice, which every day for three years had whined an accompaniment to his babyhood: "Spare a coin for the child, señor! Never mind about me, señor! Hunger has been my companion all my days. But the child, señor. . . . *Cry, you little beast, cry.*" He pressed himself farther into the dark shadow of the doorway and his aunt's voice, if it was indeed hers, faded away.

Two singing sailors, a tall man in a fez and a drunken woman shouting murderous threats appeared in succession in the pool of light outside Baldomero's, swam there through Emilio's tears like fishes in a pond, and vanished into the dark night whence they had come. Then suddenly a young girl who walked secretly like one of José's tigers slunk past the lit window and paused within a few feet of Emilio. She fumbled in her bag for a key and opened the door which Emilio was leaning against. Taken by surprise, he fell inside. The girl cried out, and as Emilio picked himself up two more girls came running down the stairs and giggled when they saw him, and dabbed his wet face with scented handkerchiefs to dry his tears and wipe away the blood. " 'Bella, 'Bella!" laughed one of the girls. "This is a fine man you've brought home with you!" They all giggled and chattered together, and the girl called 'Bella sat on the bottom of the stairs and put her arm round Emilio and drew him to her. She was warm and soft and scented, and Emilio, who had never smelt scent before nor known any embrace other than that of the gypsy's bony arms, soon ceased his crying and cuddled closer. *"Hombre! Hombre!"* crooned 'Bella, and one of the other girls asked Emilio his name, and how old he was.

"Emilio," he said, "and I am six."

"A great age," said 'Bella. "But tell me what is the matter. Why those enormous tears? Have you ever seen such tears, Juanita? They're as big as gooseberries. There, there. Tell us, little Emilio."

So Emilio very gravely described the plight of poor José, dying for lack of wine, and told how he had found his way down the Paseo de la Alameda and mistaken his way in the crooked side street, how the boot-black had run away with his pesetas and how the blind man had scratched his face.

"The old beast," cried 'Bella. "I'll never give him anything again. Why did he hit you, Emilio?"

"I think," said Emilio very gravely, "it was because I had eyes and he hadn't."

"Surely, this is a very brave boy, to run errands when he is so small," said the tallest girl, Juanita, who wore a red rose in her black hair and whose lips were as red as the flower. "We ought to adopt him, 'Bella!"

'Bella kissed Emilio on the forehead and asked him how he would like to have three sisters; and Emilio said that he would like it very much. Then all the girls began giggling again, and said a lot of things to each other which Emilio didn't understand. "Listen, little brother," said 'Bella at last, "we think you're so good at running errands for people that we're going to let you do something for us. It's very easy, and all you have to do is to play a little game. You pretend that we are really your sisters, and you go up to one of the sailors who are always walking about on the quay——"

"A fine tall sailor," giggled the girl with the flower in her hair.

"Or two or three sailors," said the third girl, "the tallest you can find!"

"And you say to them," 'Bella went on, "that you have three beautiful sisters at home and these sisters can sing and play the piano and they like sailors very much. Say also that they have plenty of wine and can cook a good supper; and then ask the sailors to come home with you and bring them here. If you do that we'll give you some pesetas to make up for the money the boot-black stole!"

"You see, it's just a game, pretending we're your sisters," explained the red-flower girl.

"But you do agree that we are beautiful, don't you?" giggled 'Bella.

"I think you are all very beautiful," said Emilio gravely.

"You'll do it then!" 'Bella clapped her hands. *"Hombre! Hombre!"* she said. "What a brave little fellow you are!"

The first sailor whom Emilio accosted on the quay wore an oily blue uniform with three rings upon the sleeves and was no less a person, although Emilio did not know it, than the Chief Engineer of a five-thousand-ton steamer, the S.S. *Loch Lomond* out of Leith. He was also a life-long teetotaller and a strict adherent of the Wee Free Kirk of Scotland. He came from Cape Wrath and his indignation when Emilio invited him to supper with his three beautiful sisters blew up like a sudden gale on that storm-swept promontory. Holding the boy by the scruff of his neck, he boxed his ears so hard that for several minutes afterwards they felt as if they were on fire; and while he laid on with a horny hand he recited in a loud and terrible voice a series of admonitions from the sixth chapter of Saint Paul's Epistle to the Corinthians. Finally he kicked Emilio upon the bottom and strode away.

After this experience it was some time before Emilio could summon up enough courage to try again; and he flitted about the dockside like a timid elf, hiding in the shadows of the cranes and packing cases, listening to the footsteps of the sailors who came and went, pouncing out to intercept them and then in sudden panic fleeing back into the darkness with his message only half delivered or not delivered at all. At last, however, the thought that José must by now be almost at his last gasp drove him in desperation to approach three drunken fellows who were staggering along arm in arm and bellowing three different songs in the belief that they were singing in chorus. Emilio followed them at a respectful distance (for his ears still smarted painfully) and attracted their attention by calling "Hi!" When they stopped singing, he recited the invitation exactly as 'Bella had told him to do:

"I have three beautiful sisters who can sing and play the piano and who like sailors very much. They have plenty of wine and can cook a good supper. They will be very honoured to entertain you if you will come home with me."

One of the sailors laughed; one said, "I've heard that story before"; and the third resumed his singing. Emilio was afraid that they were going to take no notice of the invitation, so he extemporised desperately:

"One of my sisters is called 'Bella and another is called Juanita and wears a red flower in her hair."

"Hey-ho!" said the tallest of the sailors. "And do you swear that they are very beautiful?"

*"Muy hermosas, muy guapas,"* declared Emilio with conviction; and at this the tall sailor bellowed jovially, "Then lead the way, Master Midget!" and all three started singing again. They linked arms and followed Emilio as he trotted back along the dockside; and they sang so loudly that he had no need to make sure that they were at his heels. Once, however, he nearly lost himself among the trucks and cranes and criss-crossing railway-lines; and perhaps he would never have found his way back to the house beside the wine-shop if he had not heard the faint, far crying of the lottery-ticket seller and set his course towards it. *"Loteria! Loteria!"* called the woman sadly every two or three seconds. The sound was like the moan of a fog-horn from a lighthouse in thick weather, and with its guidance Emilio piloted his sailors to harbour.

The door was opened by 'Bella, who greeted the sailors very warmly indeed and called to the other girls who emitted little squeaks of delight as they came tripping downstairs. In the excitement Emilio was nearly forgotten, but at last 'Bella pressed a silver coin into his hand and also gave him a kiss which left a scarlet smudge upon his cheek. Clutching the coin, he ran straight to the wine-shop, marched boldly up to the counter and asked the man in shirt-sleeves for a bottle of his second-best rioja in order to cure the pain in José's back. The boot-black was now shown to have been not only a thief but a liar, for Baldomero handed Emilio the bottle without question, merely cautioning him not to drop it on the way home. With the bottle cradled in his arms Emilio set off proudly down the Street of the Fourteenth of April and emerged safely at the other end of it into the Paseo de la Alameda, where he paused wide-eyed with wonder, for it seemed to him as if all the people in the world had congregated there. Bands were playing, flags were waving, and the shouting, booing and cheering was so loud that it even drowned the rattle of the trams.

"Please, señor, please," begged Emilio to a fat man who blocked his way. "I'm in a hurry. Can I get by?"

The fat man laughed.

"Well, you can get by, I suppose, if you can wriggle like an eel; but you won't get far. The whole Paseo's packed like sardines. You want to be careful, little man, or you'll get knocked down by the crowd."

"What's it all about, señor?" asked Emilio.

"Politics. You're too young to understand."

"What's politics?" Emilio asked.

"Listen," said the man grimly, "and you'll soon find out."

There was such a lot of noise going on that it was difficult to make out the words which the people were shouting; and even when he could hear them they didn't mean anything to Emilio. One section of the crowd would shout in unison:

"*Viva el Partido Obreros Unidos Marxistas!*" and the other section would then reply with a great roar:

"*Viva la Confederación General Trabajadores!*"

"Boo! Boo! Boo! *Abajo!*"

"*Arriba! Viva! Viva!*"

"Up with the workers!"

"Down with the Marxists!"

"Traitors!"

"Reactionaries!"

The shouting of these last two words became antiphonal, and with a quickening rhythm and a growing menace the yells came alternately: "Traitors!" "Reactionaries!" "Traitors!" "Reactionaries!" until the sound seemed to fill the whole universe. It became apparent to Emilio that there were two main masses of people, slowly moving towards each other, and he now perceived that each of these processions marched behind a banner. The one banner bore the legend VIVA EL P.O.U.M.! ABAJO LA C.G.T.! and the other declared VIVA LA C.G.T.! ABAJO EL P.O.U.M.! Emilio wriggled and wormed his way through the crowd on the pavement and soon found himself walking in the rear of the P.O.U.M. procession, which was going in the direction of his home. The band was playing a cheerful tune, and Emilio felt very excited and happy. Shortly, however, the shouts and counter-shouts rose to a crescendo as the two factions met head-on; there were cries of "Assassins!" "Murders!" "Down with them!" and a sudden surge of the crowd, like the backwash of a swift-running tide, swept Emilio off his feet. He rolled into the gutter, still holding the bottle in his arms, and as innumerable feet pounded about him he had time to recollect José's stories about water-buffalos, rhinoceroses, and rogue elephants. He put up his hands to cover his face and the precious bottle rolled away from him; but it was not broken, and as the running feet became fewer he dared to stretch out his hand to retrieve it. At that moment he saw, through the corner of his eye, a lean ragged scarecrow of a fellow detach himself from the crowd on the edge of the

pavement; and this fellow swooped upon the bottle like a
stooping bird. Indeed, he looked very like a bird, for Emilio,
lying in the gutter, saw him against the sky; and his rags
flapped as he pounced.

His long, dirty fingers, like talons, clutched the bottle at
precisely the same time as the boot stamped sharply on
Emilio's little hand. Then with what sounded like a squawk
of triumph he flapped away.

This time Emilio did not cry. As he sat in the gutter,
leaning against the base of a lamp-post and nursing his ach-
ing hand, a revelation came to him and he perceived in a
vague, unformulated way that the world which lay beyond
his back yard was very like José's jungle ("Tiger, see his
terrible claws!") in which predatory creatures seized whatever they desired by virtue of their strength and swiftness.

"So," he said to himself, "the boot-black was fleeter than
I, he stole my pesetas and ran away so fast that I could not
catch him. The man who descended upon me like a great
flying bird was stronger than I, so he took away my bottle
and stamped upon my hand. I see now that this is the nature
of the world."

He therefore picked himself up and made his way back
to Baldomero's wine-shop, where he acted in accordance
with the pattern of behaviour which had been demonstrated
to him. He made his way stealthily to the counter, waited
until Baldomero's head was turned the other way, laid hold
of the nearest bottle he could see, and ran away with it.

By ill-chance, however, two members of the Guardia Civíl
happened to be standing on the corner, and hearing Baldomero's shout of "Stop, thief!" they slung their rifles on
their shoulders and gave chase. Emilio had a start of thirty
yards, and now he ran (as he thought) for his very life; for

the gypsy had frequently threatened to hand him over to
the Guardia who, she said, thought nothing of cutting off
the noses and ears of little boys who misbehaved themselves.
Sheer terror sent him flying down the Street of the Fourteenth of April, with the sound of the Guardia's big boots
clanging on the cobble-stones only a little way behind him.
The soles of his feet hurt terribly, but the pain did not
stop him, and he was still a pace or two in front of his
pursuers when he turned the corner into the Paseo and
nearly collided with a man who was running hard in the
opposite direction. Emilio saw him just in time and dodged,
only to crash into another man who was following behind.
The collision sent him reeling across the pavement, but
he recovered himself and ran on for twenty yards before
he became aware that the Guardia's heavy boots were no
longer pounding at his heels. He glanced over his shoulder
and saw why. The two running men, who carried between
them the tattered remains of the banner which said VIVA
EL P.O.U.M.! were being assailed by a number of others who
strove to take the banner away from them. These other
men in turn were being attacked by an outer circle of foes;
while on the extreme circumference of the mêlée the Guardia Civíl were using their rifle-butts to bash both factions
impartially over the head. This, Emilio concluded, was
politics. He wasted no time, however, in watching the spectacle; he ran on down the promenade where everybody else
seemed to be running, and as he did so he heard, but
scarcely heeded, a succession of sharp reports like the sound
of a whip cracking. At this noise all the people in the street
began to run faster, crying, "*Caribineros! Caribineros!*" and
the promenade suddenly emptied itself as if the crowds had
been magically spirited away.

At first Emilio was only aware that there were no running

feet except his own, which being unshod made a faint padding on the pavement. Doors banged, shutters clattered down
and the lights in shop-windows went out; Emilio looked
about him and discovered he was alone. In the whole length
of the promenade nothing stirred except a mule, which lay
in the middle of the road and hammered rhythmically with
its hoofs as it died.

Panic took hold of Emilio. He had been afraid before,
of the darkness in the crooked street, of the trampling
crowd, of the blind man and of the fierce Scottish sailor,
of the Guardia Civíl; but it was nothing to the loneliness
he knew now as he stood alone under the bright lights and
imagined a thousand eyes staring down at him from all
the windows in the promenade. He began to run again,
and as he did so the mule kicked for the last time, sent a
shower of sparks flying from the tarmac, and lay still. He
fled blindly, hardly knowing or caring which way he went
so long as he escaped from the watchful silence and the
lights and the numberless eyes which seemed to burn a
hole in the back of his head as he ran; and even when he
had escaped from the glare of the Paseo he still continued
to run, and perhaps would have passed his own house without recognising it if the mongrel puppy had not happened
to jump out and prance before him, playing the bull-fighting
game, which he had taught it in the back yard.

Old José was surely dying. He hardly stirred when Emilio
crept up to his bedside, and by the light of the guttering
candle pressed the bottle into his hand. "José! José!" whispered Emilio urgently, and then the old man's eyelids
flickered, he groaned, and gradually his fingers closed about
the neck of the bottle. Emilio plucked at the bed-clothes,

and José painfully raised himself up. At last he opened his
eyes fully; he began to pull at the cork in a kind of frenzy
and it came out with a loud pop. Without a word José
raised the bottle to his lips and drank deep.

He choked and spluttered. His eyes grew wide and with
a most surprising alacrity he suddenly sat up in bed. He
held the bottle before him, blinking at it, drank again,
smacked his lips, and turned to Emilio with such a strange
expression on his face that the boy cowered away from him.

"Brandy!" said José, and took another swig.

Emilio crouched on the floor and watched José's face,
over which there crept such a look of bliss and beatitude
that it was like the spring coming upon a winter land.
"Brandy! I gave you the pesetas for rioja, and you bring
me brandy. How in God's name did you get it? *Brandy!*"
he repeated.

Emilio made no answer, and José did not seem to expect
one, for he declared happily, "I understand all. Do not
explain. It is a miracle. Say nothing. The priest once told
me it was blasphemous to attempt to explain a miracle.
I am content. My patron saint would not let me die. *He*
sent me the brandy; and you, little one, were his instrument."

José drank deeply once again, and now it seemed that he
was entirely restored to health again, for he swung his
legs on to the floor and sat on the edge of the bed. "The
saint has used you and you shall have your reward," he
said suddenly. "I will tell you a story about the jungle!"

He patted Emilio on the head, settled himself comfortably
with the brandy between his knees, and began:

"The jungle, my little one, is a very fearful place, and
extremely difficult to describe to such as you. First of all,

you must imagine it as a place where there is no law nor justice, and no rule but the rule of each for himself; and you must understand, too, that it is teeming with all manner of savage creatures, and that all these creatures are perpetually at war. There are, for example, tigers . . ."

# In Gorgeous Technicolor

*The island of Sacré Coeur, in the still-vex't Bermoothes, is* the most bizarre and the most beautiful place I have ever seen. You would expect it to be inhabited by Prospero and Caliban, with Ariel jigging about on invisible wires. Actually its population includes an assortment of ants, dozens of species of malevolent flies, innumerable mosquitoes, some sick cattle, a Welsh missionary called the Reverend Ezekiel Rowlands (Bachelor of Arts, Aberystwyth, and now minister of Capel Sion), a voodoo god called Zamballah, a couple of hundred natives mostly suffering from yaws, and a witch. There was also a little black boy called Man Friday, who was the only cheerful person in the place; but he isn't there any longer.

We called him Man Friday because he was the first human being we saw after our forced landing. We had been catapulted from our cruiser to search for a suspected blockade runner; a tropical storm had affected our compass and

we had lost ourselves. When we were nearly out of petrol
we spotted a pyramid of cotton-woolly cumulus piled up
like a snowman on the northern horizon, and it led us to
Sacré Coeur—for in those parts every islet wears its tall
top-hat of cloud. We landed in a long narrow bay which
was so crystal-clear that we could see the sharks scurrying
away before our awful and contracting shadow. When the
old Walrus amphibian came to rest, we anchored and
climbed out on the wing to have a look round. Evans, our
telegraphist-air-gunner, said sombrely:

"*Deawl!* Like the films in Technicolor, it is!"

He didn't approve of the tropics, holding that one grey
Glamorgan valley—pitheads, slate roofs, tin bethels and
all—was worth all the outlandish foreign parts that man
in his folly had ever gone on expensive pleasure cruises to
see.

He added disapprovingly, "Look at those flowers. Like
great red hungry mouths of tarts."

The jungle, multitudinously green, came down almost to
the water's edge. There was a clump of hibiscus around
which one sensed rather than saw a ceaseless flickering of
humming-birds. Great patches of orange-red cassia exploded
like bomb-bursts at night. On the fringe of the jungle
flamed dozens of Flamboyant Trees. As Evans said, it took
your breath away; but if you saw it on a picture postcard
you'd think it a bit vulgar. Timothy, my observer, exclaimed
suddenly:

"Hello! Here comes Man Friday!"

During the glide down I had noticed cultivations, and a
few buildings huddled around the next bay to the north.
Man Friday now came running round the promontory
which divided this northern bay from ours. He was aged
about seven, jet-black, and entirely naked. Instead of follow-

ing the curve of the beach he plunged into the water and took a short cut by swimming. He swam extremely fast, using an effortless crawl. Approaching us, he disappeared under water and finally came up beneath our starboard wing. He shook his black frizzly head, grinned, and shouted:

"Hello, Jo! Throw penny!"

Tim found one and tossed it towards him. The boy turned a somersault like a gobbling duck, kicked his little pink heels in the air, and down he went through the clear water in which the penny gleamed and flashed as it sank towards the bottom. His small fist shot out to secure it, and he rose grinning and spluttering, trod water under the wing, and yelled:

"'Nother! Throw penny, Jo! Throw 'nother penny!"

We spent about sixpence on his antics, in spite of an uncomfortable feeling that we might be sacrificing him to the sharks; but perhaps they were harmless, or feared our aeroplane, or respected small boys who could swim almost as well as they could. Anyhow, they kept away.

There now appeared, walking round the promontory, a group of the island's sedater inhabitants. They were led by a tall, elderly white man who wore an alpaca coat, grey flannel trousers, and a panama hat. We waded ashore to meet them, pursued by Man Friday, whose insatiable desire for pennies suggested that the island was at least civilised enough to possess a sweet shop.

It was certainly civilised enough to possess a church; for the tall white man explained to us that he was the minister. "I have but a small flock," he said, with a slight conventional smile, "and mostly black sheep in it," and he indicated the handful of starvelings who stood unsmiling (and, it seemed to us, unwelcoming) behind him. "And it is a far cry from Capel Sion on the mountain, and the long grey

valleys, and the Eisteddfodau. But I like to think that the
Lord has work for me here."

"What part of Wales do you come from?" asked Evans
eagerly.

"Brynmawr. My father was Rowlands Postmaster. But
that was long, long ago. It is like—like looking in a glass
darkly. I have lived on Sacré Coeur for twenty years."

"Twenty years!"

The old man nodded.

"And never before," he said, "never in twenty years,
have I had visitors out of the sky. You are welcome."

We experienced great difficulty in sending a message to
our ship. ("Full of gremlins the bloody wireless is," chanted
Evans, "and the whole Fleet will be searching for us, and
they will send a telegram to my mother to say that drowned
I am!") But at last we got in touch, and Evans told the
cruiser our tale of woe. She replied rather tersely that she
would "proceed to position indicated and embark us in a
few days' time." Apparently she was busy hunting the blockade runner. Our captain hated aeroplanes anyhow, and
probably felt that he was well rid of us. We wondered
whether he knew that Sacré Coeur was inhabited, or whether
he imagined we were living on coconuts.

We heaved the Walrus up on the beach (assisted, of
course, by Man Friday, who crawled about inside the fuselage and nearly set off the fire extinguisher), and then we
walked round the promontory to the minister's bungalow,
where he had invited us to stay. Man Friday led the way,
chasing long-tailed butterflies along the fringe of the
jungle. The Reverend Ezekiel had gone ahead to prepare
for us.

On the way we had a curious and rather uncomfortable

encounter. We met a woman of about forty, who was walking in the opposite direction, and as we passed her she was smiling, but not at us. She was tall and striking-looking, and she wore flowers in her hair, but her eyes were feverish in the hard, cruel face, and she walked gracefully and wickedly, as a cat walks. Tim said, "She gives me the creeps," and I nodded.

Man Friday, butterfly-hunting, had lagged behind, and we saw the woman stop and speak to him. He ran away from her, crying, and came to us as if for protection. He was whimpering like a frightened dog. We asked him what the woman had said and who she was, but he would not answer. She walked on and disappeared from sight around the promontory; and soon Man Friday dried his tears, though he didn't chase butterflies any more. He stayed close to us. Evans said surprisingly, as if it were the most natural thing in the world:

"She was a witch, didn't you realise?"

"What nonsense, Dai!" I said.

"We have witches in Wales, too," he said complacently.

We went our way, and came to the bungalow.

If you saw a picture postcard of it, you would remark on the charming contrast which the pretty whitewashed bungalow made with the bright-green foliage behind it; on the little wooden church, incongruous perhaps but rather gallant, standing in its small triangular clearing hard-won from the jungle, and on the mass of multicoloured flowers which formed a kind of hedge round church and bungalow alike. I had never seen so many flowers, so closely packed together, except at a graveside. But they were not all flowers, for as we approached, a number of them took wing, detached themselves, and flew away. Man Friday, his fears forgotten, ran off in pursuit.

Yes: the minister's bungalow would look very nice on a picture postcard, with the biscuit-coloured beach in front of it lapped by the deep blue sea, and the cassia and the hibiscus and the great tawny tiger-lilies. But the postcard wouldn't show the flies, the mould, the marching ants, the ceaseless pinging mosquitoes; and in the picture those great trees, the jungle's outposts and advance-guards, would look benevolent and sheltering, instead of suffocating and malign.

One had a dreadful feeling, in that bungalow, that one was cornered, surrounded, and invested by the jungle. It was closing in all the time. It infiltrated, it crept in unseen and unheard. Its poisonous breath, clammy, steamy, all-pervading, seeped through floor-boards and skirtings and walls, condensed on the tables and chairs, blurred the windows, made the sheet on one's bed feel as cold as a shroud. *"All the infections that the sun sucks up,"* said the Reverend Ezekiel, who had a trick of apt quotation and a lot of untidy scholarship. Our white shoes were covered with bright green mould every morning. How they grew, those moulds! The invisible spores of the fungi came in with the wind and the rain. A slice of bread left on the table overnight would be furred with long green penicillia next day; a fresh mango, in a few hours, would be turned into a mass of mushy slime.

Then there were the ants. "I have seen them marching in the jungle," said the Reverend Ezekiel, "and I have been sinner enough to question God's purpose in creating so many. I have seen the monuments they raise to themselves, structures taller than a man, and I have reflected that they may be more permanent than my own Capel Sion." Sometimes they marched out of the jungle and invaded his territory. The cruellest thing they had done was to destroy, in a night, more than half his precious store of books. Plato,

Shakespeare, the *Mabinogion,* were empty shells; the bindings remained, but their hearts were eaten out. You opened *Romeo and Juliet* and the printed page crumbled away before your eyes; as transitory, as impermanent, as love itself.

"Anything you value," said the Reverend Ezekiel, "should be placed on a table and the legs of the table stood in pails of water. Fortunately the creatures cannot swim."

There were other enemies. One looked inside one's shoes in the morning lest a scorpion lay hidden there. One walked delicately for fear of snakes. A myriad assorted flies assailed one. And there were the mosquitoes.

"I used to be very careful about them," said the Reverend Ezekiel. "I used to take precautions." He shrugged his shoulders. His shaky hand, his wasted frame, told the rest of the tale. "But you get tired," he went on. "Tired of draining ditches and pouring paraffin into puddles. And one night there is a big tear in your mosquito net, but you are tired, and you say to yourself: There are a million harmless ones to each anopheles, and even anopheles can't hurt one unless he has bitten somebody else who's got it. And you lie in bed, and you hear *ping! ping! ping!* and you think of those comforting odds—but somehow the Theory of Averages doesn't seem to work out."

His malaria recurred, now, every rainy season. He had grown resigned to it. But even in between bouts he wasn't as fit as he used to be. Things that once were easy had become too much trouble. His little bit of cleared land, held on sufferance from the jungle, had already begun to dwindle. Locusts had destroyed the flower-garden in which, he told us proudly, an English rose had precariously blossomed seven years ago. The pathetic pretence of a lawn had withered and disappeared in a month of drought; and during the subsequent rains the jungle made a sudden sortie

and recaptured the carefully dug-up patch where he used
to raise English vegetables. He was too tired, too weak,
to counter-attack. "The vegetables were never much good,"
he pleaded. "The peas were luxuriant, but they had no
flavour. The potatoes were huge, watery, and soft. And
it's difficult to get the seed, anyhow, in war-time."

So he let the jungle consolidate its gains. It advanced a
few yards farther, constricting him, trying to squeeze him
out. A Fifth Column, consisting of enormous yellow fungi,
had already established itself outside the front door. In
Capel Sion itself the tendrils of some vigorous vine were
pushing up through the wooden floor. The Reverend Ezekiel
lopped them off every few days; but it made no difference:
they soon grew again. He routed up their roots; but new
shoots appeared next morning. *"Naturam expelles furca,"*
he quoted with a shrug and a smile, *"tamen usque recurret."*
That summed up his attitude to the jungle now; he didn't
fight it any more, he accepted it. "How it grows!" he exclaimed wearily. "How literally it obeys God's command:
'Be fruitful and multiply!' Yet I have dared to wonder,
sometimes, whether this prodigality comes of God or the
Devil. A cancer, they say, is caused by normal cells running
riot and multiplying unreasonably. I have often wondered
whether, in the jungle's crazy growth, there is not something
cancerous. Those great fungi like yellow cheeses; those parasitic orchids with wicked yellow flowers!" He shuddered.
"It is all so fierce, so violent, so uncontrollable. If you make
a solid concrete floor, the plants will burst up through it;
and only the other day I heard a sharp crack and discovered
that a tree had thrust its branch clean through the window-
pane. Yet I had lopped that tree only a few weeks previously.
*Tamen usque recurret!"*

He went about with a pair of garden clippers, vaguely and

ineffectually cutting off the shrubs, boughs and weeds which had ventured farthest into his domain; but he might just as well have tried to lop off the tips of the tentacles of an octopus. We used to watch him, pottering about with his clippers, and Tim christened him "the blind Fury with the abhorréd shears." That was a pleasant quotation, but it didn't fit, for there was nothing like that about the Reverend Ezekiel. He was a pitiful, weary, sick and frail old man. The island of Sacré Coeur was no place for him and no place for Capel Sion. I had a fantastic and rather uncomfortable notion that one day the greedy jungle, which already so closely invested him, would surge forward and swallow him up—Capel Sion, bungalow and all. I had that feeling very acutely on the third evening of our stay, when the swift dusk had gathered about us and the great trees at the end of the garden seemed terribly close, seemed to be creeping forward in a solid phalanx, and then suddenly I heard the voodoo drums beating on the hill.

At first I was only vaguely aware of them—*beat, beat, beat,* at the back of my consciousness—they were just a different noise from all the previous noises. For that was another oppressive thing about Sacré Coeur: it was never silent, there was never any stillness or hush. All day you were irritated by the ceaseless dry shrill telephone-wire noise of the cicadas. Then, towards dusk, that noise merged into the innumerable chirping of crickets. ("Yes," said the Reverend Ezekiel, "one grows tired of them. The grasshopper shall become a burden, you know.") At dusk the cricket's chirruping merged into the deep-throated muttering of frogs, like the conversation of disgruntled clubmen.

Then, when the evening shower was over, the chorus of strange anonymous night-creatures began: whoops, howls, hisses, hums. And now this new noise, deep, loud, rhyth-

mical, beat its way into our consciousness and became a
background to our talk; but our host had no half-remem-
bered tag, no apt quotation, this time. He fell silent, and
the noise of the drums rushed in to fill the silence, like air
into a vacuum.

Evans went hurriedly on (they had been talking about
Wales):

"And Jones Tackleshop married the eldest daughter of
Roberts Red Lion, the public house on the corner between
Capel Bethesda and Griffiths Shopdraper . . ."

But the Reverend Ezekiel wasn't inclined to indulge in
local reminiscences any more. He said shortly, "Yes, indeed,"
and then suddenly he got up.

"Forgive me," he said, "if I leave you. I always spend
Friday evening preparing my sermon for Sunday; it avoids
a last-minute rush on Saturday. Good night."

He went out. We heard his old, tired step going down
the corridor towards his study. I wondered what sort of
a sermon he would write, and how many or how few would
listen to it in Chapel on Sunday morning. It occurred
to me again how very frail the old man was, how precariously stood Capel Sion. The Latin tags, the rusty scholarship,
the scraps of assorted wisdom from the Old Testament and
Shakespeare, didn't avail him here, provided no answer to
the terrible logic of the jungle and the dark questioning of
those voodoo drums. And what of the God of the slate-
coloured valleys, whose temples were tin bethels four thousand miles away: did His writ run, I wondered, on Sacré
Coeur?

Tim said slowly:

"D'you know, I don't like this place. I can't think why,
but it gives me the jim-jams. I shall be glad when the ship
comes and we can get away."

"It was your phoney navigation that brought us here," I said.

"Yes, I shall be on the carpet before the captain, I expect. But I shan't mind if only we can get away from here soon. What are those drums?"

"Some voodoo nonsense going on."

"What do they do?"

"Chop off the head of a white cockerel in a magic circle; and dance; and drink bad rum; and work themselves into a sort of hysteria. If they're feeling very naughty they may even kill a goat. It's all silly nonsense really, Tim. Not wicked, just silly."

Evans said:

"In Wales we have foolish superstitions also."

"I saw the witch again to-day," Tim said. "Oh—I meant to tell you. It was rather odd. She was talking to Man Friday. They seemed great pals. Yet he was so scared of her the other day."

"Perhaps she's discovered that the way to his heart is to throw him pennies," I said. "Though I can't see what she wants with him."

Evans, whose profounder observations always sounded the weightier by reason of their curious inversions, pronounced gravely:

"Perhaps a child of her own she does desire and cannot have. Very strange and pitiful such women are. Barren cows they do resemble, that nuzzle another's calf. Such a one there was in the town of Pontypridd . . ."

Evans related everything to Wales.

"Well," said Tim, "you may be right; but I don't like her; and I don't like this island; and I don't like the noise of those drums. Before they turn me into a Dancing Dervish, I'm going to bed."

So we turned in, and through fitful slumber I heard the drums going all night. I thought I heard singing too; but perhaps I dreamt that. When I woke up the sun was bright in the burnished sky, and the cicadas filled the air with a sound like wind through dry bamboos.

We had an arrangement with the ship that we should keep a listening watch on the wireless during certain hours of the day, in case she had any message for us. This was Evans's job, but usually we all went down to the beach with him. I would fiddle about with the engine, and Tim would lie in the sun and play with Man Friday.

But when we strolled down to the aeroplane next morning, Man Friday didn't come with us. At first this didn't strike us as unusual, for he sometimes joined us later, appearing mysteriously out of the jungle or, having swum round the promontory, out of the sea. One day he had arrived in lordly fashion on a donkey which later, driven mad by flies, kicked a dent in the fuselage of the Walrus. On another occasion he had spent the whole of a hot forenoon riding round in small circles on a bicycle with two flat tyres. He was an enterprising child.

"He'll probably turn up in a Rolls," I said to Tim.

But the day wore on and there was no sign of Man Friday. We went back to the bungalow for lunch and returned to the beach in the afternoon, because it was cooler there. I was lying drowsily on the sand with Tim, and watching through half-closed eyes a great metallic blue butterfly, as blue as a piece of the Virgin's snood, sail beautifully along the fringe of the jungle past the scarlet flowers, when Tim said suddenly:

"I'm worried about that brat, Johnnie."

Tim loved children: he was a bit of a child himself, impressionable, mischievous, and playful. The beach still bore traces of the sand-castles and moats, the dams and canals, which he and Man Friday had constructed yesterday.

"Perhaps he's sick," I said, "or his parents won't let him come out."

"He hasn't any parents. He lives with an old crippled aunt who doesn't bother about him. His Reverence told me."

"Well, it is a bit funny," I said.

After a few minutes Tim got up.

"I think I shall go back to the village and have a look for him."

I stayed in the shade of the Walrus's wing and dozed. It was more than half an hour later when Tim woke me up.

"Johnnie," he said urgently.

"Yes?"

"I've been all round the village and I can't find the brat. I asked everybody I saw but they couldn't tell me anything. Or they wouldn't. They were odd, very polite and non-committal, and sort of cagey. They put on blank faces; I thought they knew more than they'd say. Then I met that fat boy who's not quite right in the head. I asked him, and he laughed. Then he said, 'He's gone up the hill with Her.' I said, 'Who's she?' and he just laughed and wouldn't say any more."

I sat up.

"Well, what are you worrying about? Perhaps he likes witches. Perhaps the witch gives him more pennies than we do." But he still looked unhappy. "What's the *matter*, Tim?" I said.

"I went to see his Reverence," said Tim, "and I didn't like what he told me."

"What did he tell you?"

"I started off by asking about the witch. He looked very

uncomfortable and said, 'Yes, yes, poor woman,' two or
three times. 'Perhaps she is a *little* strange,' he said, 'but
she has had a great sorrow. Recently she lost her husband.'
I said, 'I should think he was well out of it,' and old
Ezekiel nodded. 'She's a difficult creature and there was—
er—domestic trouble.' I asked him to tell me about it. He
said, 'There was—er—a girl involved. Even on Sacré Coeur
we are not without our—er—moral lapses.' "

I interrupted.

"Tim," I said, "what is this extraordinary story all about?"

"Please do listen. I butted in: 'So he got tired of his
witch and ran off with another girl? I can't say I blame
him,' and His Reverence nodded and muttered, 'It is not
for us to judge, indeed; and the poor man is dead. *Nil
nisi bonum.*' After a bit of prompting from me he went on:
'His death was a great puzzle to us,' and I said straight out,
'Did she murder him?' But no, it was nothing like that,
he said. The man just died. He didn't have fever, he didn't
have T.B., he just wasted; and when he was very ill they
sent him away in a schooner to the big hospital, but the
clever doctors there couldn't do anything for him. And
after he was dead they made an examination and they
couldn't find out what he had died of. That's all."

Evans had crawled out of the fuselage and joined us. He
said:

"Indeed there was a witch at home who got rid of her
husband in just the same manner. It is a spell they do put
upon them. But in this case it was not because of the
adultery. A different motive she had. That the poor man
no longer would make love to her the reason was."

We laughed; but Tim still looked worried. I said:

"All right, Tim. Perhaps she did kill her husband. Perhaps she made a waxen image of him and pricked it with

pins. And he *thought* she'd put a spell on him, so he died from fright. It's an old story. But there's no reason why she should harm a child."

"Perhaps not. All the same"—Tim frowned—"when I was talking to old Ezekiel I had a feeling that he was worried too, but he wouldn't admit it even to himself. I think he's a brave and good and obstinate old man who's trying hard to pretend that some of the things which happen on this island don't really happen at all. If he didn't pretend he'd go mad; because he'd have to admit that his twenty years of hell here have been wasted." Tim put his hand on my shoulder and added seriously, "Johnnie, don't you, too, sometimes have that feeling about His Reverence— that he's deliberately shutting his eyes to things because he's lost his nerve?"

I'd had exactly that feeling, on the previous night, when we listened to the voodoo drums. I had thought: The old man is pretending he doesn't hear them. So I knew what Tim meant now. He was an imaginative boy; he was quick to sense things. Already he knew more about the island and its uncomfortable "atmosphere" than I or Evans did. I asked him:

"What do you want to do about it, Tim?"

"I want to find Man Friday. I want you two to come with me, up the hill. I know where the place is. Will you come, Johnnie?"

I nodded, and we got up.

We passed through the village, and we saw the Reverend Ezekiel pottering about with his shears, trying to chop down a very tough vine which had a stranglehold on the front porch. We didn't ask him to come with us; he was too old and sick to climb the steep hill.

We went up by a path over which the trees met, roofing it like an alleyway. It was dusky and still, and had the queer damp smell of a hothouse. The path was well trodden by many feet. Then we came out into a small clearing where a fallen tree was speckled with huge parasitic flowers. Tim said:

"There are two ways here. We don't want her to get away, so we'll do a pincers movement. I'll take the high road, and you take the low road; and we'll arrive at the top simultaneously. Infantry Training Part One."

Tim seemed excited and nervous. I could sense his anxiety, though I thought he was making too much of the whole business. He climbed up the steeper of the two tracks; Evans and I followed the other one. It took about twenty minutes to get to the top.

There was a big clearing here, carpeted with long grass which had been trampled down in places. There were two or three bamboo huts, and in the middle of the clearing was Zamballah's altar. We found the cold ashes of a fire.

But there was nobody about. It was very still, and the sun was setting and the wind had fallen. The only sound was a ceaseless hissing and rustling in the grass, where snakes or some small creatures moved away from our footsteps. The jungle cast long black shadows over the clearing; and through the trees to the westward we could see the blaze of the sinking sun, like a city afire.

We heard Tim coming up the path.

"Nobody here!" we shouted. Tim came through the long grass towards us.

"I know," he said. "I met her on the way down."

"The witch?"

"Yes. I suppose I was wrong. I suppose I shouldn't have taken any notice of that idiot boy. All the same, I wish we could find the kid."

"He wasn't with her?"

"No. She was by herself. I asked her whether she'd seen the boy; and she said yes, she'd seen him this morning. He followed her for a bit and then went off chasing butterflies. She smiled—you know the way she smiles—and it irritated me, so I got tough and said, 'What are you doing up here anyhow?' 'Picking mangoes,' she said. She'd got a basket, with a banana leaf on top. I pulled off the leaf—I don't know why—she couldn't carry Man Friday about in a basket. I think I expected to find a white cockerel for the sacrifice or something."

"Well, what did you find?" I asked.

"Mangoes. Just a few squashy mangoes."

"While we're here," I said, "we might as well have a look round. Have you ever seen a voodoo altar, Tim?"

"No. It doesn't look very impressive."

Tim went across to look at the *hounfort*. I thought I'd take a glance at the bamboo huts. I went into the first one and found nothing but a heap of empty rum bottles which had contained the dangerous, raw local spirit they call *Mal cochon*. (I don't know why, unless it makes you a "bad pig" if you drink it!)

The second hut was tumbledown and disused; and the third had a hole in the back through which the sunset-light filtered and made a rose-red pool upon the floor. By that light I saw the small dark bundle in the corner.

Man Friday looked smaller than ever in death. He felt as light, when I picked him up, as one of those little gazelles which flit through the jungle undergrowth. I carried him out, and called Evans and Tim, and we uselessly loosened the thin cord which had strangled him. I didn't realise, till Evans exclaimed, what else they had done. Then I noticed the blood on my hands and saw the long tear in his chest: like a stab-wound, only much neater and tidier and much more purposeful. And Tim cried out, something about "The basket!" and still I didn't understand. Tim was very white. "Oh God," he said. "Those mangoes." And then the crazy horrible truth flooded in on me, and I knew the reason for the island's name.

"Leave the body where it is, touch nothing, and ring up the police": but you can't do that on Sacré Coeur. There is no telephone and only one policeman, and he lives at the other side of the island, four miles by the rough jungle track, and he, no doubt, is a pillar of the Law but he also has a wholesome fear of witches.

So we wrapped Man Friday in a coat and carried him down to old Ezekiel's bungalow. It was dark already, and there was no point in chasing the woman; we should merely have lost ourselves. So we sent Ezekiel's servant across the island to fetch the policeman. He came back three hours later and told us, "Sergeant gone fishing in boat. Come to-morrow." It might have been true; but it was more likely that the Sergeant had funked walking through the jungle at night. The jungle must be very frightening if you believe in Zamballah.

After dinner we sat uncomfortably and miserably with Ezekiel, not knowing what to say. Slumped in his chair, haggard and silent, he looked more than ever worn-out and broken. But he was still obstinate; he would not tell himself, he dared not tell himself, the dreadful truth. Once I asked him outright:

"Why did the woman take the little chap's heart?"

He shook his head.

"Terrible, terrible," he said. "But she is mad. We must always remember she is mad. We can't look into the minds of such people."

"Don't you think," I asked, "that your villagers believe there's some special magic in a heart?"

"No, no. A horrible notion. But inconceivable. Not here. They are poor and sick and ignorant but they are not— not idolaters."

I dropped the subject; it would have been cruel to go on. Soon afterwards he went to bed, and I lay awake for a long time listening to the unfamiliar silence. Not wind nor thunder nor rain stirred the breathless air. The frogs made no sound. There were no voodoo drums, no songs; and the villagers stayed indoors. It was the first time I had known stillness on Sacré Coeur; and I did not like it.

Next morning, Sunday, we expected the policeman but he didn't come. At ten o'clock Ezekiel rang the cracked, rusty bell which sounded more like a warning of shipwreck than a summons to prayer, doors began to open, and in silence the villagers trooped to Capel Sion.

I stood watching them, and wondering how much they knew and how much they guessed, when suddenly Tim shouted and pointed across the bay.

"Look! The ship's come for us!"

She stood off-shore, hove-to, about three miles out; apparently the navigator mistrusted the shoals. Soon she would lower away the motor-boat, to tow the Walrus out to her. There wouldn't be much time to get ready.

So we hurried back into the bungalow and packed our things, and then went into the chapel to say good-bye to our host. To our dismay the service had already started. The little chapel was full; we had to stand up at the back, and by craning our necks we could see Ezekiel's weary, ravaged, ascetic face. He was just finishing what I suppose was a short address. I don't know what it was about but the last sentence made me shudder. *"For He knoweth the secrets of the heart,"* quoted Ezekiel. He paused and repeated sternly:

*"For He knoweth the secrets of the heart."*

There was a small, tense, audible sigh, as if the congregation caught its breath. Then there was a short silence. Ezekiel stood there, frail and gallant, his head bowed, and I pitied him and feared for him. Then he gave out the number of a hymn, and I was aware again of the hiss of indrawn breath, a tremulous sigh, and of an atmosphere of suppressed excitement which distracted and disturbed me. The hymn started, and I had a chance to whisper to Evans:

"Is it making you homesick? Is it like Capel Sion at home?"

Evans said shortly, "There's something wrong."

I knew that. But it was only during the second verse of the hymn that I understood exactly what it was. I glanced at the people nearest me, and I suddenly became aware that the words they were using were not the words of the hymn. As my ear became adjusted to the singing I realised that almost the whole congregation was chanting in Creole. Perhaps, I thought at first, they have their own version of that old hymn. But there was a hysterical note in the singing, there was a faint shuffling sound which grew louder —as feet began to move and bodies to sway. I glanced at the woman on my right and saw her fingers twitching at her breast, at the man on my left and saw his back and shoulders rippling. I looked at their faces and suddenly I became aware of the truth which old Ezekiel dared not tell himself.

I had guessed it before; but my guess had just missed the mark. I had imagined Capel Sion as threatened by the

jungle, and I had seen a symbol in the vine's long tendrils
which even now were intruding through the windows and
getting a grip on the inside wall. One day, I had thought,
the jungle will swallow up Capel Sion. And when I had
listened to the voodoo drums, I still thought of the affair
in terms of a conflict between Capel Sion and ancient magic
—on the one hand, Zamballah; on the other, poor Ezekiel.
I thought that the drums were a challenge; and feared lest
they, and the bad local rum, might incite the villagers to
burn down the little wooden church, because Zamballah
would tolerate no rival on his island.

But now, as I listened to the fervent singing, and heard
the rhythm break and change, and the confused shuffling
of feet merge into a regular stamp, stamp, stamp, which
dreadfully echoed the remembered beat of the drums—
now I knew that there was no conflict any longer. The
jungle had already entered Capel Sion, and Zamballah had
triumphed. He had no need to destroy the precarious
wooden church; for he could be worshipped there as freely
as he was worshipped at the *hounfort* on the hill.

I touched Evans's arm, and Tim's, and they nodded, and
we went out into the sunlight. The motor-boat was close
inshore, heading for the bay beyond the promontory; so
we hurried down to the beach, and as we ran along the path
hedged with beautiful and terrible flowers we could still
hear the singing in Capel Sion, where a hundred people
chanted a hymn to Zamballah and one frail, brave, foolish
old man blindly and obstinately praised God.

# Mr. Catesby Brings It Off

*The nights grew cold after his wife ran away, so the Captain* courted the blonde barmaid from the Lion, and soon he took her home to his semi-detached on the cliffs overlooking Swansea Bay. To the neighbours he described her as his housekeeper; but the term had come into disrepute lately through a mistake on the part of a local weekly, which had printed an elderly farmer's advertisement for *Housekeeper, single, 25—30, strong, cheerful, willing,* in the column headed LIVESTOCK AND PETS. So the neighbours disbelieved the Captain's story, and their giggles and gossip hurt his pride. He bought a remote little farm among the mountains, at a place called Cwm-y-Rwyddfa, and settled down there with his girl. He arranged to have her surname changed by deed poll, and innocently supposed that everybody round about would assume that she was his wife. Far from it: the postman, the policeman, the Minister from Capel Bethesda and an R.S.P.C.A. inspector known as Roberts the Cruelty

who came prying round and accused him of starving his
cows—all in turn took it for granted that he was a widower
and that Myfanwy was his *daughter*. Once again his dignity
suffered—but in silence; he was too proud to argue with
strangers about his private affairs. So the matter went by
default, and the girl remained his daughter as far as Cwm-y-
Rwyddfa was concerned. This did not displease Myfanwy,
who would smile to herself about it now and then.

Captain Salvador Miguel Meredith-Jones was at that
time a man well into his fifties, hawk-nosed and handsome,
not unlike the pictures of Satan in Victorian editions of
*Paradise Lost,* but with a large black moustache, which he
touched up with a little dye whenever it showed signs of
becoming grizzled. His mother had been Spanish, and he
had never forgotten the language which he learned at her
knee; he had a great store of its proverbs, which he translated for Myfanwy's benefit. She didn't much like them,
for they were what she called "sarky." He knew Spain well,
for his Welsh father had owned three small steamers which
carried coal to Gibraltar and brought back ore from Huelva,
olive oil from Malaga, oranges from Almería. Salvador himself had gone to sea when he was sixteen and had got his
Master's ticket before he was thirty; but when his father
died, leaving him a little fortune, he immediately retired in
order to "look after his money." He looked after it so well
that his wife, fed up with his cheeseparing, went off with
an open-fisted bookie who crumpled pound notes into little
balls and stuffed them into his trouser-pockets.

The Captain had refused to divorce her, detesting equally
scandal and expense. In all respects he became increasingly
mean; but this troubled Myfanwy less than you might think,
for she was a young woman who took the long view: the
less he spent now, the more there would be in the bank

when he was gone. She noticed that he became chesty in
the cold weather and coughed dreadfully at night. His heart
was apt to pitter-patter, he said; and she remembered him
telling her that his father had gone sudden, with his heart.
She suggested calling a doctor, but he quoted one of his
Spanish proverbs: " 'God cures the patient, and the medico
pockets the fee.' " Later that evening he suddenly quoted
another: " 'More people have died because they made their
will than because they were sick' "—which caused Myfanwy
a moment of dismay, for in her mind she had been buying
herself a nice little house not too far from the lights of
London, and a leopard-skin coat, and a Mini, and a pleasure
cruise in a liner, where sitting at a cocktail bar or splashing in a swimming-pool she would at last meet him whom
they called Mr. Right in the women's magazines.

Meanwhile, however, she was not discontented with Cwm-
y-Rwyddfa farm. She'd been brought up in the country; and
now she milked the cows, fed the pigs, and looked after
the chickens. When two of the ewes died, she enjoyed bringing up their lambs on the bottle. As for the Captain, she
was quite fond of him in a way, despite his meanness and
his sarkiness now and then. She was a little frightened of
him, too, which made life less dull than it would otherwise
have been at Cwm-y-Rwyddfa.

Indeed, the couple might have continued to live there
happily until death them did part; but for one of the cows
falling sick, and the Captain ringing up the new young
vet rather than the old one, because he reasoned that he
might be both cheaper and more up-to-date.

A glow of yellow lamplight in the windows of the farmhouse gave it an air of comfort and homeliness which ap-
pealed to the young vet, who knew little of either. He lodged

with a gaunt and bearded female called Mrs. ApHugh who treated him not half so well as her yapping Peke Chinky or her cat Tibb. She would slap down before him a tepid pot of tea and a nearly cold plate, covered by a quite cold plate, enclosing a small piece of fatty bacon and a broken egg fried into a beige-coloured shapeless slab, and she would say in her menacing fashion, "There's your breakfast, Mr. Catesby, and I trust you'll have no niggling complaints this morning." Then almost in the same breath she would coo to the cat, "Did it want the top of the milk with all the lovely cream on it then?"

This morning Mr. Catesby had missed his breakfast altogether. He had been called to a calving case, and when he got back it was too late even for the fried egg. "You cannot expect to treat my house as a hotel, Mr. Catesby." As he set out empty-bellied on his rounds, self-pity seeped through him with the dank November cold. He thought of all the things he would say to the bearded hag if ever he won a football pool. He cursed the lazy old skinflint for whom he worked as Assistant with a View to Partnership—if indeed he could ever afford to buy his share of the practice. He coveted the luck of film-stars and heavyweight boxers and playboys who married heiresses. He gave himself indigestion with resentment and envy, and with the lumpy cheese-sandwiches he gobbled for lunch. At three o'clock he rushed back to his Small Animals Clinic, which he hated because he'd acquired a distaste for small animals through his acquaintance with Chinky and Tibb. Then, just as he was looking forward to thawing out his legs before the gas-fire in his digs, the surgery telephone rang and a man with a damnably imperious voice was saying, "This is Captain Meredith-Jones of Cwm-y-Rwyddfa." Another of those Welsh tongue-twisters! Mr. Catesby hated Wales because it was

the native land of Mrs. ApHugh. "Spell it, please," he said,
and the man did so, then pronounced it syllable by syllable
as if to a child.

And here it was, ghost-grey in the fading light, lonely at
the top of the valley between the steep hills; but it looked
wonderfully welcoming to Mr. Catesby as he went up to
its front door. He could smell bread baking, and he wondered whether he would be offered some tea. If a man
had a pretty young wife for company, he thought, one who
could bake and roast and make a Yorkshire pudd., crisp on
top and soft inside like his mother had done in Huddersfield;
it wouldn't be a bad life, even in this back-of-beyond. He
was impressed by the contrast between the farm's snug security and the wildness of the surrounding hills. He would like
to lie in a feather-bed cosy beside that Yorkshire-pudding-
maker and, as he cuddled her, hear the bitter wind blowing
round the chimney-pots.

So he was thinking, when the door was opened and there
stood just such a plump and cosy girl as might indeed have
warmed a man at the chilliest season! Because of what was
in his mind he felt himself blushing, and she stared at him
in surprise, as if to say: "The new young vet! Goodness how
shy!"

"This is Captain Meredith-Jones's?" he stammered.

"Of course. And you have come to see the cow." Already
she was kicking off her shoes and stepping into a pair of
gumboots. "She calved yesterday morning quite easy; today
she went as if she was drunk, wild-eyed like, and now she's
down on her side, and all blown up her stomach is, her legs
sticking out straight and stiff . . ."

She led Mr. Catesby out to the stall where the Friesian
lay. He leaned down and passed his hand in front of her
eye. The eyelid did not move. Coma. Milk fever.

"Nothing much to worry about," said Mr. Catesby. "I'll have her up within an hour."

Most of the farmers he dealt with believed they knew more than he did; and they were probably right. He would have been less than human if he had lost this chance of showing off a bit in front of somebody who might be impressed by his professional skill.

As he opened his leather case and brought out the big syringe, the girl stood close by his side, attentively watching him; and suddenly he was surprised by a powerful whiff of scent, unexpected at any time in a cow-shed and quite without precedent in the working life of Mr. Catesby, which was accompanied by a mixed aroma of disinfectant, pungent animal medicines, and muck. He was so excited that he feared she would see his hand trembling as he prepared to inject the cow. It was all he could do to keep his mind on the job. When it was done he glanced up and found himself looking straight into the girl's eyes. Her frank gaze, and the smile that went with it, gave him a confidence which he generally lacked.

"You'll see. She'll be as right as rain in less than an hour," he boldly predicted, adding rather grandly as he put away the syringe: "Calcium boroglutinate"—a sonorous phrase. Myfanwy continued to gaze at him admiringly.

"You'll be wanting to wash your hands," she said at last. "And of course you'll stay to tea."

She led him back into the house, and left him in the wash-place while she put the kettle on the kitchen-fire. Then she took him into the parlour, which was just as he had imagined it would be, as warm as his lodgings were cold. Birch-logs crackled on the fire, and a big oil-lamp cast a kindly glow upon the azure backs of the stuffed kingfishers, the copper-lustre china, the row of Toby jugs, and the

sailing-ship-in-a-bottle which had pride of place of the
mantelpiece. A pipe-rack on the wall reminded Mr. Catesby
of the owner of the house.

"Is your father not in?" he asked; and he failed to notice
her moment of hesitation before she replied:

"I expect he's gone down the paddock to shut up the
hens. The foxes have been terrible about here ever since
the myxie . . . I'll go and make the tea." And she gave him
a look over her shoulder which warmed his spirits quite
as much as the fire was warming his legs.

How cheerful the pictures were!—mostly of blue seas and
foreign parts—much nicer than the yellowing photograph
of the late Mr. ApHugh as a Royal and Ancient Buffalo
which hung upon the wall in his digs. A painful and des-
perate longing for domesticity nearly overcame Mr. Catesby.
The new-bread smell, as Myfanwy entered with the tray, did
nothing to assuage it. There was farm butter, with little
drops of moisture glistening on it like tears of joy where
the pat had been cut in two! There was home-made black-
berry jelly, with the jar labelled in a girlish hand *B. Jell. 64.*
There was a generous globular old-fashioned teapot clothed
in a thick, quilted tea-cosy obviously tailored to fit it, for
the short brown spout protruded out of it like the head
of a well-rugged horse.

During tea, when he wasn't looking at Myfanwy, Mr.
Catesby's eyes would dwell upon this object, and he would
reflect sentimentally that the very word "tea-cosy" seemed
to epitomise his present situation, which he wished could
continue for ever.

"How the days do draw in!" sighed Myfanwy at last. "Pull
the curtains I must." She got up to do so, and with the
idea of helping her Mr. Catesby got up also. As they stood
side by side at the fireplace he was enveloped once more

in her attendant aura of scent. In a new access of nervousness, he picked up the ship-in-the-bottle and pretended to
study it.

"Was your father perhaps a seafaring gentleman?"

After an imperceptible pause she nodded.

"I've heard they tie a piece of thread to the mast," he said,
"and when they've got the ship inside they pull this thread
and up goes the mast and all the rigging."

"Really?" said Myfanwy in her most ladylike voice. Peering hard into the bottle (though she could scarcely have
been less interested in anything), she half leaned against
him, and Mr. Catesby was aware of her thigh pressed against
his, soft as that quilted tea-cosy save for a sharp knobbly
lump which he supposed to be something to do with her
suspender-belt and which therefore lent a fearful intimacy
to their juxtaposition.

At that very moment the door opened and the Captain
took two long dramatic strides into the room. He carried
a hurricane lantern, in which the flame flickered as he swung
it. His moustache alone was enough to alarm poor Mr.
Catesby, who upon his entrance had jumped at least a yard
sideways. Myfanwy had done much the same thing in the
opposite direction; and of course this sudden flying-apart
made them look very guilty and feel very foolish indeed.
Mr. Catesby still clutched the ship-in-the-bottle, and juggled
with it awkwardly as he prepared to offer the Captain his
right hand. As for Myfanwy, her agitation was pitiful to see.
She blushed and she trembled. Mr. Catesby had heard of
Victorian fathers ready to horsewhip any of their daughters'
suitors of whom they did not approve; and since Wales in
his view was not so much Victorian as medieval in its cus-
toms, he was quite prepared to believe that the terrible
Captain, with his blazing eyes and his fierce moustache,

might be a tyrant of that nature. To his still greater alarm,
the man now addressed him in a foreign tongue. What the
Captain actually said was:

" '*Quien arecha por agujero, ve su duelo.*' "

After a suitably impressive pause he translated it for his
hearer's benefit. Myfanwy had already guessed that it would
be sarky. It was.

" 'He who spies through a keyhole will see what will vex
him,' " said Captain Salvador Miguel Meredith-Jones.

There was a silence during which the hurricane-lantern
popped and flickered; Mr. Catesby dared not look in the
direction of Myfanwy; and the Captain's formidable moustache seemed to twitch as he treated them both to a tigerish
smile. At last he spoke again:

"Well, Mr. Catesby, you are a quick worker," he said.

More terrified than ever, Mr. Catesby was moved to justify
himself. He always stammered at moments of stress; he was
now so foolish as to try to explain, in a series of stutters,
that he and Myfanwy had been studying the problem of
how ships got into bottles. It made no sense at all, and the
Captain cut him short with a gesture.

"I was referring, sir, as it happens, to your *professional*
skill. The cow is on her feet. Excellent. No doubt in due
course I shall receive your bill."

He held open the door; and with the merest shamefaced
farewell glance towards Myfanwy, Mr. Catesby took the
hint and shuffled through.

A couple of months went by before Mr. Catesby received
his second summons to Cwm-y-Rwyddfa farm. In the circumstances he was surprised, though gratified, to be asked
there again. He concluded that he must have made a better
impression on the Captain than he had supposed; con-

veniently forgetting that his desire to see Myfanwy again had induced him to send a ridiculously small bill for his previous visit.

On this occasion his patient was a pig; and once again Mr. Catesby was fortunate. He hadn't the faintest idea what was the matter with the animal; for pigs were puzzling in their ailments, and in Mr. Catesby's experience one could only be quite sure of one's diagnosis if the trouble was a broken leg. This pig, however, ran fast on all four legs when Mr. Catesby, syringe in hand, pursued it round and round its muddy pen. Once he slipped down in the mud, and caught a glimpse of the Captain's sardonic smile. He was glad Myfanwy was not watching. Catching up with the pig at last, he pumped into its backside a large dose of penicillin; and with a confidence he was very far from feeling he said to the Captain:

"I think you will see a great improvement tomorrow."

Next evening Myfanwy rang up to tell him that the pig had quite recovered. He was really the cleverest vet. The Captain, she said—and in his excitement at hearing her voice he failed to notice that it was an odd way to speak of him —the Captain was shutting up the ducks. "We can have a good natter." They did.

It turned out to be a rough winter and a tardy spring. The Captain's half-starved animals were perhaps more subject than most to the ills attendant on bad seasons; or perhaps—since Mr. Catesby now refrained from sending him any bills at all—the Captain was not averse to taking advantage of a free veterinary service. And with what glad haste Myfanwy would rush to the telephone whenever the Captain told her, "Send for the vet"! Their romance blossomed and thrived against a background of weirdly-named animal ailments, such as pulpy kidney, twin-lamb disease, louping ill,

and orf. They held hands behind hayricks and snatched
kisses in cow-sheds. Upon one or two occasions when the
Captain was up on the mountain looking to the sheep they
made still better use of their opportunities, for Myfanwy
had discovered that her bedroom-window gave an excellent
view of the hillside opposite; at the cost of no greater dis-
traction than a quick glance now and then, you could reas-
sure yourselves that he was still half a mile away. His
thin and spavined pony was by no means up to his weight.
The mountains were steep. It was surprising what a lot of
ground love could cover while he covered a mere half-mile.

Myfanwy had very little difficulty in finding excuses for
her deception. For one thing, he was fifty-five. Couldn't help
it, but a man ought to regard himself as past it at fifty-five.
For another thing, love justified all; and Myfanwy had
persuaded herself that she was very much in love. Maybe
Mr. Catesby wasn't *exactly* the image of Mr. Right that
she had conjured into her daydreams; he had, for example,
a tendency to spots, especially on the back of his neck
between his rather close-cropped hair and his collar. But
this was a small consideration in relation to the fact that
he was the only male under fifty whom Myfanwy saw for
months on end.

As for Mr. Catesby, his ardour in courtship had been
reinforced by a piece of intelligence which came to him by
chance through a friend who worked in a lawyer's office.
This young man, more callow and even spottier than Mr.
Catesby, was the only person in the world who looked
up to him; they used to spend Saturday evening together
drinking beer and talking about girls, especially the wantonness of girls, of which they knew much by hearsay. Now
that for the first time Mr. Catesby had experience of this

wantonness, no wonder he boasted about it to his admiring friend, who at the mention of Cwm-y-Ryddfa immediately pricked up his ears.

"Meredith-Jones?" He dropped his voice to a whisper. "Well, if that isn't the miserable old skinflint who came into our office to make his will the other day. He's got oodles of money, my boss says; and won't spend a bean. I had to make a copy of his will; promise you won't breathe it to a soul if I ——"

"Promise!" said Mr. Catesby breathlessly.

"Oodles of money; and he's left it all to his daughter! The farm and everything, the whole caboosh. If you've wangled your way in there," said Mr. Catesby's friend, goggle-eyed at the thought, "I can tell you you're on a jolly good wicket, old man!"

After that, you may be sure, Mr. Catesby was troubled less often by his trifling fastidious wish that Myfanwy had been, say, about seven years younger; and he was able to put out of his mind altogether such pernickety preferences as he had for brown eyes rather than blue; for long thin legs rather than short plump ones; and for straight dark hair rather than frizzly blonde hair which looked as if it might have been dyed.

On a blue morning in the very early spring, when the first lambs were white specks all over the far mountainsides, Myfanwy rang up Mr. Catesby very excitedly and told him: "He's gone off to market for *the whole day* . . . And the baby ducks have got the sprawls," she added as an afterthought. "I think you'd better come out quickly and see what you can do about the sprawls!"

So the young vet in his old car drove so fast to Cwm-y-Rwyddfa that the radiator was spouting like a whale long before he got to the top of the pass between the mountains.

At the farmhouse he was greeted by the delicious smell of a stew cooking and a strong whiff of Myfanwy's scent; in combination they provoked a confused reaction, by no means disagreeable, of amalgamated passion and greed. Myfanwy when she had kissed him nodded in the direction of the kitchen and smiled slyly: "It's the remains of the Sunday joint. I'll have to tell him the cat got it—the old meanie!" She had discovered the key of a locked cupboard from which she had filched a bottle of Spanish wine. "He'll never notice it's gone." On the laid table there was a crusty loaf and a large pat of butter, yellow as marsh-marigolds, and some Caerphilly cheese. There was a bowl of walnuts, of which Mr. Catesby was inordinately fond.

"I thought we'd have a feast," said Myfanwy. "Just you and me. But there's plenty of time before the stew's done. We mustn't waste it."

Nor did they. Indeed, by the time Myfanwy turned her thoughts once again towards the oven, the stew was so overdone that most of the meat was stuck firmly to the bottom of the casserole, and the onions and carrots had gone dark brown. However, they were able to sort out a few edible pieces, and by the time they had drunk the whole bottle of wine between them Myfanwy was apt to get the giggles whenever she thought of the reason why she had let the stew burn. Mr. Catesby spread the deep-yellow butter on slice after slice of bread, balanced on top of it a good lump of cheese, and thought of Mrs. ApHugh's stale loaf and her mean portion of marge. Then he started on the nuts, and cracked some for Myfanwy, and soon they went over to the sofa by the fire, where they nibbled and canoodled, and Mr. Catesby thought sentimentally that marriage must be rather like this, a matter of eating and cuddling in endless permutations. So he plucked up his courage and then and there invited Myfanwy to marry him.

"Say yes, and I'll ask your father the moment he comes back from market!" cried Mr. Catesby.

Her response to this suggestion surprised him. At first she giggled; then she squeaked in what seemed to be genuine alarm. When she squeaked she struck a note that was nearly as high as a bat's squeak.

"Don't you dare say a word to him ———"

"Why ever not?"

"He'd be wild at you. I don't know what he'd—*No!*" squeaked Myfanwy in growing agitation. "*No! No!* I can't explain. You wouldn't understand . . ."

"Of course I understand," said Mr. Catesby soothingly, slipping his arm once more round her plump waist. "He'd be very sorry to lose you and I don't blame him either. We must try to win him round together. We must somehow put it into his head that what he needs is a *good house-keeper*———"

At this her squeak became so high that it seemed to ping upon Mr. Catesby's eardrums, and then like the bat's squeak it went out of his sonic range altogether. Instead, another sound suddenly impinged upon his ears. The front door opened, and very quietly shut. The Captain had come back early from market.

Myfanwy leaped to her feet.

"I will ask him now," said Mr. Catesby, made bold by half a bottle of rioja, rough but strong. Myfanwy then seemed to lose her nerve altogether, and as the Captain entered the room she dodged round behind him and bolted through the door like a rabbit. Mr. Catesby listened to her footsteps, none too light, thumping rather than pattering up the stairs.

The Captain glared at him.

"Well, Mr. Catesby," he began, "which of my animals are you attending to today?"

Mr. Catesby had struggled up from the low sofa; he knew his mouth was smothered in lipstick and he must look like a clown. He sought refuge from his absurd situation in an absurder formality.

"I am glad you have come home, sir, because there is something I have been wanting to say. I wish to ask you for—for——" He blushed and hesitated, and remembered the phrase which he'd read in some old book; ridiculously it sprang to his lips: "—for Myfanwy's hand in marriage."

The Captain's eyes opened so wide that Mr. Catesby could see the whites all the way round them. He took a pace forward, threateningly. His angry stare travelled from Mr. Catesby to the empty bottle on the table, to the remains of the meal, then up to the ceiling. From Myfanwy's bedroom came a faint hysterical sobbing.

The Captain's stern silence became unbearable.

"I expect—er—you had lunch in town?" said Mr. Catesby, desperately trying to make conversation. Then he wished he hadn't, as the Captain picked up the casserole and examined it curiously.

"My mother's people have a proverb," he said at last. " 'Love is a furnace, but it does not cook the stew.' However, they have another saying, 'There is no sauce like a good appetite.' Pray be seated while I put it to the test."

The wretched Mr. Catesby sat down on the extreme edge of one of the chairs which was drawn up to the table. The Captain fetched himself a knife, fork and plate, and took the place opposite him. He helped himself to some small pieces of the stew, turning each one over several times to see whether it was composed of burnt meat or burnt carrot. As he did so, Mr. Catesby in awful fascination watched his moustache twitching like a cat's whiskers.

Meanwhile the Captain was thinking fast. The girl was a slut. *Twitch.* She was deceitful. *Twitch.* She was not all that to look at, she was getting blowsy, she was Letting Herself Go. *Twitch.* She was a petty thief. *Twitch.* She was improvident with the housekeeping money and incapable of understanding that saved pennies added up to pounds. (How often had he quoted to her his dear old mother's precept: 'Grain by grain the hen fills her crop'?) The Captain tried to make a calculation in his mind, setting the few amenities provided by Myfanwy against the expense of keeping her. He discovered a debit balance; and promptly he made up his mind.

"Call the girl down," he said to Mr. Catesby.

Mr. Catesby went obediently to the door and shouted up the stairs:

"Myfanwy! Your father wants you."

The Captain grinned tigerishly to himself. Mr. Catesby returned, there were galumphing footsteps up above, and shortly Myfanwy appeared, dabbing her face with a powder-puff.

"Come here," commanded the Captain, so sharply that her bottom waggled agitatedly as she hurried into the room. Her tight skirt was rucked up on one side and hung down on the other. One of her stockings sagged. The Captain observed her contemplatively. He eased himself back in his chair.

"Mr. Catesby has informed me," he began, "that despite appearances to the contrary his intentions are entirely honourable. I understand that he wishes to marry you; and I have decided to give my permission and—er—my blessing. In the cupboard from which you took the rioja you will find also a half-bottle of Spanish champagne. Kindly fetch it."

Myfanwy's mouth made a perfect "O" but no sound came out of it. She turned to Mr. Catesby, she turned back to the Captain. "Fetch it," he barked again. "And bring three glasses." Myfanwy's "O" grew larger and larger, but if she squeaked it was another of her supersonic ones.

*"WHO giveth this woman to be married to this man?"*

One had to admit, thought Myfanwy, as she peeped side-ways at the Captain through her veil, that it was wonderful how he had come round to it. There must be some good in him really, for who'd have thought he'd have hired the village hall and laid on a reception for nearly twenty people, eats and all—and him so mingy? Who'd have thought he'd have bought a dozen bottles—well, not of champagne but of champagne cider, which was the same colour and had the same sort of fizz, so that if you took the labels off nobody would know the difference? He'd even asked one or two of his relations to the wedding, because Myfanwy, who was an orphan, hadn't got any of her own whom she was very proud of, and it wouldn't look well if all the guests belonged to the bridegroom's family.

Myfanwy hadn't yet met the Captain's relations. She be-lieved he had a brother and sister still living; and that dark pretty girl whom she'd caught a glimpse of as she walked up the aisle—she was probably his niece.

"To have and to hold from this day forward, for better for worse, for richer for poorer," her bridegroom was mum-bling. His Yorkshire accent was more marked than ever, because he was so nervous, she supposed. Even in this mo-ment of solemnity she was aware that he wasn't Mr. Right *exactly*. Unfortunately, he had acquired a large new spot.

it might even be an incipient boil, on the left side of his
nose, just in time for the wedding. A quick peep round her
veil showed Myfanwy that it was even bigger than it had
been yesterday. He was making heavy weather of the things
he had to say. Myfanwy confessed to herself that he hadn't
got much gumption. When they started married life in the
little semi-detached he'd rented, she was the one who'd have
to tell him how to go on. And that'd be a change, thought
Myfanwy, after life with the Captain, who during their very
first week together had repeated to her seven times one of
his sarky proverbs. She had heard it so often that she knew
it by heart: "Sad is the house where the hen crows and the
cock is silent."

But the old misery must be rather fond of her, she thought,
in spite of his sarkiness. Otherwise he wouldn't have left
her all his money—and she knew there was a hell of a lot of
it in the bank. The farm and the furniture too: "the whole
caboosh." That was the phrase Mr. Catesby had used. She
would scarcely have believed it if he hadn't told her that
he had it straight from the lawyer's clerk, his best pal, the
one who stood beside him now, fumbling for the ring—
goodness, he was feeling in both his pockets, he looked pretty
wet; she hoped he hadn't lost it!

With all that money, she thought, life with Mr. Catesby
would be very tolerable, whether he turned out to be Mr.
Right or whether he didn't.

She took another timid peep through the left side of
her veil. The Captain, she decided, was looking rather old,
and not at all healthy.

As he fingered it nervously at the reception, Mr. Catesby
became quite certain that the new spot on the side of his
nose would indeed turn out to be a boil. He could read
it with his fingertips as a blind man reads Braille; he had

vast experience of boils. The suspicion that he was going
to take one with him on his honeymoon had already driven
him to drink half a dozen glasses of the champagne cider,
which far from cheering him up seemed to leave as sour a
taste upon his spirit as it did upon his tongue. Not even
the whispered encouragement of his friend the best man—
"Never mind, old chap, at least you've landed her"—did
much to comfort him. Nor did the Captain's proposal of the
Happy Couple's health. Myfanwy had warned him it would
be sarky, and it was. She reacted with nervous giggles,
either through nervousness or because she'd had too much
to drink. In Mr. Catesby's ears they were as shrill as the
squeals of those little pigs upon which from time to time
he performed a small necessary operation. The Captain,
who had heard the sound many times before, winced. He
looked rather sadly towards Mr. Catesby and quoted another
of his depressing proverbs:

" 'For a marriage to be happy the husband should be deaf,
and the wife blind.' "

This provoked much laughter from the wedding guests,
who seemed to have reacted more happily to the cider than
Mr. Catesby had. The best man, chuckling most tactlessly,
took him by the arm and said:

"He's certainly a card, the Captain . . ." He dropped his
voice. "More to him than you'd think. They say he actually
kept a *liebeside*—may still do, for all I know. *At his age!*"

The awful import of this was at first lost upon Mr. Catesby;
for he had just caught sight of a girl, at the other end of
the room, who was tall and slim, with long slender legs,
and very dark straight hair, and dark dramatic eyes. She
was so much the embodiment of all he desired in womankind
that it was as if he were looking at a dream come to life. He
fixed his gaze upon the exquisite creature and he could not
take it away even though he knew that Myfanwy by his

side was glaring at him resentfully. He did not notice the approach of the Captain, whose grating voice close at hand brought him to his senses suddenly.

"Very pretty girl, eh?" remarked the Captain, "though I says it as shouldn't. I must bring her along and introduce you. I know you'd both be interested to meet my daughter ——"

"Your—your—*what?*" gasped Mr. Catesby.

"Only child . . . my wife and I . . . parted a few years back . . . faults no doubt on both sides," murmured the Captain, who was in a very good humour and could afford to be generous. "Yes, my daughter. You can see the Spanish blood coming out in her, can't you?"

"*Daughter!*" cried Myfanwy suddenly in her very shrill voice, seizing her husband by the arm and squeezing it so tight that he could feel her sharp fingernails digging into his biceps. Once again her mouth made a big "O," in which condition her whole face became far from attractive and she appeared to have several double chins. She turned away from the Captain and towards Mr. Catesby. The Captain studied her expression with lively interest. She seemed to be seeing, not only her husband's present boil, but a lifetime of boils; and what was much worse, a lifetime of boils without any money.

The Captain took his eyes off her, and went closer to Mr. Catesby's side. Paternally, affectionately, indeed almost gratefully, he laid a hand upon his shoulder.

"My mother's people have a saying: '*Si tu mujer quiere—*' but you don't know the language, of course. My daughter over there—Consuela—she speaks it like a native. I'll put it into English. The saying runs: 'If thy wife tell thee to throw thyself from a balcony, pray God it be a low one.'"

And the Captain smiled his tigerish smile.

# The Octopus

*On the twenty-first of October,* for goodness knows how many years, the four Old Comrades had dined together at the Hotel Lion d'Or. They were survivors of the famous 133rd Division, known as La Gauloise, and the excuse for their celebrations was no less than the immortal victory of Verdun. It was proper therefore that they should dress themselves for the occasion in white ties and tail-coats, with the season's last roses fading in their buttonholes, and feast upon the tenderest young partridges prepared as only the chef of the Lion d'Or knows how. It was fitting also that they should drink to the memory of generals and *poilus* impartially in the best Bordeaux wine. And, if not fitting, it was very natural that they should fall into passionate argument about the strategy and tactics of the battle, quarrel, come to blows, forgive each other, embrace, weep, order more brandy, sing the Marseillaise, and tell each other repeatedly what fine rip-roaring old soldiers they were, until

at last in the small hours they were escorted home by the
proprietor, the chef, and the night-porter and delivered over
to the wrath of their outraged womenfolk.

  Next morning, sick and soreheaded but with the consciousness of glory and splendour not yet departed from them,
they slipped back unobtrusively into the routine and rhythm
of their lives. Sebastien stood contritely behind the counter
of his grocer's shop; Lucien screwed up his courage to enter
the strong-smelling factory where he made Camembert
cheese; Marcel with something less than his usual air of
importance lorded it over the young women who sold ladies'
underwear in a drapery store. Only Jean-Baptiste, who was
a bird of passage, escaped the good-humored badinage of
friend and neighbour; for already his Amusement Fair was
rumbling away down the long, straight road, whence it
would return exactly a year later, predictable as a planet,
to set up its stalls and its roundabouts in the Fair Ground
at the back of the hotel.
  The years went by, the Old Comrades grew greyer and
fatter, more pompous, more respectable, and Verdun faded
into a confused memory of their late teens; but the annual
celebrations were sanctified by tradition, and only death,
they swore, should bring them to an end. So even when
Lucien became Mayor of the commune, with Marcel and
Sebastien as his deputies, they booked their accustomed
table on the twenty-first of October, ordered the wine and
the partridges, dressed themselves in their glad rags, and
made their way at seven o'clock to the Hotel Lion d'Or.
Jean-Baptiste's roundabouts were blaring out their ten-
year-old tunes, the Great Wheel spun merrily above the fairground, and some yet bigger contraption, like an enormous
swing, rotated behind the hotel's chimneys. The familiar

medley of shrieks and giggles, music and machinery, stirred
ancient memories and Lucien shook his head sadly.

"Too old for such goings-on, eh, Sebastien?"

"Alas!"

"Yet I can remember the time," said Marcel with a glint
in his eye, "when I could make the girls giggle on the
swings . . ."

The others sighed and nodded; and Sebastien said gravely:

"It is particularly important, Lucien, that we should remain sober tonight, you being Mayor."

"It is imperative," said Lucien sternly.

"Absolutely essential," said Marcel.

Nevertheless, a few moments later, they were drinking
Pernod in the bar and ridding their memories of certain
winged words shouted after them by their wives as
they left home. Before long, Jean-Baptiste joined them,
having done the rounds of his Fair to make sure that all was
going well. He came blustering in like a breath from the
wider world, full of funny stories about lion-tamers, dwarfs,
monstrosities, and the Fattest Woman in France who was
one of his latest acquisitions; it was nine o'clock before they
sat down to dinner. An hour later the partridges were
finished, and the table was littered with bits of bread,
knives, forks, spoons, matchsticks and cigarette-packets dis-
posed to represent the crumbling front of Verdun which
had never quite crumbled away. Soon it occurred to the
Old Comrades to reinforce this front with balloon glasses
of brandy, indicating the heavy artillery behind the lines;
and Sebastien employed a bottle of claret to demonstrate
his company's assault upon the fort of Vaux. Lucien saw fit
to observe that the assault had been somewhat half-hearted;
whereupon Sebastien lost his temper and began wildly to
wave his arms. *"This* is how we took the fort of Vaux!" he
shouted, and swept the bottle into Lucien's lap.

The old waiter, hurrying to the rescue with a napkin, was not in the least surprised: something of this sort had happened on every previous anniversary—and it was not for the first time, either, that Marcel as he watched the purple stain seeping over the tablecloth observed sententiously:

"Like blood. Blood. Ah, my friends, how it flowed at Verdun!"

At once all was amity. Lucien and Sebastien embraced each other, tears streamed down their faces, the waiter brought another round of brandy and Jean-Baptiste began to make the speech which he always made about eleven o'clock in the evening:

"Shoulder to shoulder we stood," he said "and shoulder to shoulder we stand tonight. *Vive La Gauloise!*"

They gulped down the brandy, and as soon as the waiter had brought some more Jean-Baptiste was on his feet again.

"I give you the toast of General Passaga."

Soon they were drinking toasts so fast that they lost count of them; for half an hour they were the friendliest fellows, the greatest cronies, the staunchest comrades in the world —and then suddenly they were the bitterest foes as Lucien rose from his chair, white and trembling with rage, seized Jean-Baptiste by his coat-lapel, and accused him of proposing the health of Marshal Pétain. This also had happened before, and the old waiter shrugged his shoulders, unmoved. Jean-Baptiste, it was well known, had made a lot of money during the Occupation, for he could scarcely forbid the German soldiers to ride on his roundabouts or prevent them from paying twenty-five francs to gape at the Fattest Woman in France. Thus he had laid himself open to the terrible charge of collaboration. To tell the truth neither Sebastien, Lucien, nor Marcel had resisted the Germans very actively. Sebastien had continued to sell his groceries, Lucien to manufacture

his cheese, and Marcel (when nobody was looking) to tickle
the ribs of his young saleswomen, just as they had done in
peace-time. But all three of them, when they were drunk,
believed themselves to have been the most stout-hearted
Resisters, members of the Underground, associates of the
Maquis; and therefore the very name of Pétain was enough
to start a quarrel.

"I heard you distinctly," said Lucien, shaking Jean-
Baptiste violently by the collar.

"I swear to you," choked Jean-Baptiste, "that I said nothing of the kind."

"You did. I have two witnesses."

"No."

"Liar."

"Dog."

"Collaborationist."

"I merely said, 'Let us drink to the Marshal.'"

"Ha-ha! But your exact words were, 'To the old Marshal.'"

"There are many old Marshals."

"Indeed? Then be good enough to tell us *which* ——"

"Marshal Ney! Marshal Soult! What does it matter which
old Marshal I had in mind? They are equally heroes—
Marshal Murat, Marshal Jourdan, Marshal Benadotte,
Marshal Foch——"

"Poof. They are all dead."

"And so, my friends," cried Jean Baptiste, at his last
gasp, "are most of the comrades to whose unfading memories
we have been drinking tonight."

"Alas! How true!"—and in a trice Lucien was embracing
Jean-Baptiste, Sebastien was shaking the hand of Marcel,
and the four Old Comrades stood shoulder to shoulder
once again.

"Let us," said Jean-Baptiste magnanimously, after he had

ordered some more brandy, "let us for a moment change the subject. My modest little Fair, as you have doubtless noticed in the past, has always prided itself on being up-to-date; and this year I have had the privilege to bring to your town, for the first time in history, a wonderful—I nearly said a miraculous—machine. . . ."

Now until this moment the celebration had followed exactly the same course as all the previous ones; and without doubt, if Jean-Baptiste had not innocently mentioned his new machine, the whole hotel would have shortly been awakened by a drunken chorus singing the Marseillaise and the proprietor, the chef, and the night-porter (who were already standing by) would have escorted the Old Comrades home. Save for a headache or so, nobody would have been any the worse in the morning. It was Jean-Baptiste's changing the subject that caused all the trouble. A tradition was broken: that they should talk and argue about nothing but Verdun; and from that breach, as you shall see, flowed the most appalling consequences.

"—It names itself the Octopus," said Jean-Baptiste impressively; and ordered the waiter to bring another round of drinks.

"The Octopus? Why?" asked Lucien.

"Because, my old friends, the thing has eight arms. Eight arms composed of the most perfectly tempered steel, which as a matter of fact I bought at a high price in the black market—they originally formed part of a British Bailey bridge. Now these arms revolve——"

"Ah yes, I remember," said Marcel hazily. "Behind the chimneys. I saw them. Like a swing."

"Not in the least like a swing," declared Jean-Baptiste with dignity. "Nothing so old-fashioned as a swing, I assure you. These arms, as I was saying, revolve in the horizontal plane around a great pillar of steel, weighing nearly a thousand kilos, and are driven by an engine of unbelievable horse-power, which as it happens I obtained by greasing the palm of a colonel in the Army: it once provided the motive power for no less than a German Tiger Tank."

"Very remarkable," interrupted Sebastien, "but what's the thing *for?*"

"Permit me to explain. At the end of each of the steel arms is a miniature carriage, just big enough for two. These carriages have plush-upholstered seats and although I am under an oath not to divulge how I obtained them, I may as well tell you that they were manufactured from the wreckage of a first-class sleeping car. They rotate——"

"You are making my head go round," complained Lucien.

"So would my machine! They are fitted with fins, or shall we say little sails, like a windmill's, which cause them to rotate upon their own axis while the steel arms of the Octopus revolve around the central pillar. There is, moreover, a further ingenuity. A gear of incredible complexity, which once operated the steering of the tank, causes the steel arms to rise and fall as they rotate. So you have this marvellous situation: the inhabitants of the little carriages are spinning like tops, at thirty revolutions to the minute, while *simultaneously* they are hurtling through the air, now skyward, now earthward, at the speed of an express train. You comprehend?"

"By no means," murmured Sebastien thickly. "You sound as if you were trying to explain the solar system."

"But of course!" Jean-Baptiste seized a bottle and some brandy-glasses and began to arrange them upon the table. "You have taken the words out of my mouth. The miraculous machine is a solar system in miniature. *This*, see"—he indicated the bottle—" is the central pillar. Let us call it the sun. These are the little carriages revolving about it and spinning as they go." There was a sharp crack as Jean-Baptiste snapped the stem of a brandy-glass. "My machine," he ended grandly, "imitates faithfully the ro- rotary motion of the earth."

"Poof!" exclaimed Lucien. "It is nothing. At this very moment *I* am on the earth, spinning and revolving, and I don't need to pay through the nose for the experience."

"Have another drink and you'll spin a bit faster," suggested Sebastien.

Marcel, meanwhile, stared owlishly at the circle of brandy-glasses, thought hard, and pointed a pudgy finger at the bottle in the centre.

"Where," he demanded, "is the moon?"

This was too much for Jean-Baptiste. They were barbarians, cretins, ignoramuses, imbeciles, he declared as he jumped excitedly to his feet. They were blind to the wonders of science, and in their folly they mocked at the miracles of modern engineering. Nothing would content him but that they inspect the machine themselves. There it stood, in the fairground at the back of the hotel. No small provincial town had ever before been given the privilege of seeing such a machine.

"Come!" he said, seizing Marcel by the coat-collar. "Come!" he cried, pulling Lucien up by his hair. "Shall it be said that such a phenomenon appeared in your town and the Mayor himself was unaware of it? Fie!" declaimed Jean-Baptiste at the top of his voice. "What will the citizens say tomorrow, when everybody is talking of the wonder of the great machine and, lo, the Mayor alone proves to be ignorant of it!"

Thus by heaving and exhortation he succeeded in raising

Sebastien and Lucien to their feet; and Marcel contrived
to get up under his own steam. For a few moments the Old
Comrades stood together in a confused huddle, each sup-
ported by the rest, so that it seemed to the waiter that if
one of them detached himself all would go down in a heap.
Jean-Baptiste, however, still retained the power of command
which had made him a lieutenant at the age of twenty.
*"Vive La Gauloise!"* he cried in a great voice; and at the
sound of that ancient battle-cry his companions rallied as
they had rallied thirty years ago before the blazing ruins of
Douaumont. They braced their shoulders and held their
heads high, and their uncertain feet even contrived somehow to keep in step as they followed Jean-Baptiste past the
wondering waiter and out of the room.

The church clock struck one as the Old Comrades entered
the fairground and paused for a moment to collect their
wits at the foot of the Great Wheel. The stalls and the
merry-go-rounds had closed down at midnight and there
was not a soul to be seen. Jean-Baptiste explained that his
people would have to be up at dawn, getting ready for the
road, and so were snatching a few hours' sleep in their
caravans parked around the town square. He was familiar,
no doubt, with this unnatural quietude of the slumbering
Fair; but the others, for whom the Fair was inseparably
associated with blazing jazz and whirring machinery, chatter
of cheapjacks and shouting of crowds, were somehow put out
by the silence and looked about them in fuddled wonder
at the rampant heraldic beasts on the merry-go-rounds, frozen
it seemed into pieces of statuary even as they pranced and
cavorted; at the tall tower of the chute which looked like
a winding staircase to the stars; and at the long steel arms
of the Octopus which raftered the sky and palely glinted

in the light of the full moon. They were puzzled, too, by a curious noise which alone broke the silence, a sound that rhythmically rose and fell, becoming now the faint sobbing of the wind in the trees, now the deep contented purring of a lion that has made its kill. There was something ghostly about it and they glanced at Jean-Baptiste uncomfortably, but he shrugged his shoulders and smiled:

"It is the Fat Woman. She sleeps and snores."

There was a chilly wind blowing out of the north, and instead of sobering them it had had the opposite effect. They clung to the girders which formed the framework of the Great Wheel, and when they looked upward they could almost imagine that it was going round. Sebastien shuddered and muttered something about, "Wouldn't care to be up there"; but Jean-Baptiste with an easy air of proprietorship slapped the uprights with his hand and then put his shoulder against them, so that the whole contraption rattled and shook.

"Very old machine," he said. "Getting unreliable. Last week it stuck."

"Stuck?" said Lucien.

"With one of the most influential citizens of Lisieux perched in the topmost basket," grinned Jean-Baptiste. "Devilish awkward. He remained there all night."

"All night?"

"And there was his wife screaming and dancing round the foot of the wheel and swearing that she'd have me for damages."

"Did you have to pay?" asked Marcel

Jean-Baptiste gave a sly wink. "Not I. He would almost have been willing to pay *me* for the experience. His young secretary was with him in the basket. That was what all the fuss was about. I didn't realise it at the time; I thought

he was alone; but every now and then I noticed a slight—
how shall I put it?—a slight unaccountable tremor in the
whole machine; and whenever that happened the wife would
start screaming and abusing me afresh. Hey-ho!" sighed
Jean-Baptiste, and chuckled deeply. "A showman's life is
full of variety! But follow me, my friends, and let me show
you the incomparable machine, the masterpiece of modern
engineering, the wonderful Octopus. *Vive La Gauloise!*"

He led them between the empty stalls and the silently-
prancing horses on the roundabouts towards the middle of
the fairground, where the central pillar of the Octopus rose
up as straight as a poplar and four times as thick; but their
progress was slow, because Lucien and Sebastien kept tripping over tent-pegs and guy-ropes and Marcel could hardly
be dragged away from a tent which bore the legend PARISIAN
STRIPTEASE on a placard decorated with the pictures of several naked girls. "Are they inside?" he asked hopefully; but
Jean-Baptiste protested that they were asleep in their caravans, each one defended by her mother. "Truly formidable
women, the mothers are," he said.

"But the Fat Woman—*she* does not sleep in a caravan?"
argued Marcel; and indeed it was clear that the Fat Woman
lay very close at hand, for the sound which had seemed like
the sough of the wind was now like the whistling of a bomb
as it descends, and the sound which had seemed like the
purring of a lion was now like the deep-throated gurgling
of an enormous whirlpool.

"One hundred and sixty-four kilogrammes," said Jean-
Baptiste. "It would take a wagon to shift her. She sleeps
where she works." And indeed as they passed the tent of
the Fattest Woman in France they saw the canvas alternately
bellying outwards and contracting inwards, systole and
diastole keeping time with her snores.

"Hush!" whispered Jean-Baptiste. "I would not have her awakened for anything. It is like a pig, you comprehend? The more they sleep the fatter they get. Tread softly as you pass her door."

A few moments later, however, despite his protests, the Old Comrades were kicking up enough noise to wake the dead. They had come across the miniature shooting range and had insisted that Jean-Baptiste should turn on the lights. Their rifle muzzles traced arcs and circles in the air as they blazed away at the targets; it was a wonder they did not shoot each other. Even Jean-Baptiste picked up a gun and joined in the fusillade.

"Shoulder to shoulder," he said, "as we stood as Verdun."

"And do you remember," said Lucien, "how the Posen regiments came against us, in grey-green waves, and we fired till the cocking-pieces of our rifles burned our hands?"

"I can almost see them in the sights now," cried Lucien. "Down with the Boches!"

"*Vive La Gauloise!*"

The sound of the shots, and the feel of the rifle-butts against their cheeks, polished up their faded memories until they were so bright they seemed to belong to yesterday; thirty years vanished in a flash, and once again the Old Comrades were defending the sacred soil of France against the brutal invader. "Shoulder to shoulder!" choked Jean-Baptiste, overcome with emotion; and immediately the others threw down their rifles and embraced him, patted him on the back and kissed him on the cheek, and declared that never in all the long history of arms had old soldiers been bound by such inseverable bonds of comradeship and devotion. So deeply moved was Marcel that he burst into tears, and the sound of his sobs formed a treble accompaniment to the snoring of the Fat Woman, who as it happened

had once slept all though an American air-raid and was not
to be awakened by anything so trivial as the rattle of
musketry.

"But come!" said Jean-Baptiste suddenly, wiping his
eyes. "We waste time. The latest mysteries of modern engineering are about to be unfolded to you. What are you
waiting for?" He linked arms with Lucien and Sebastien;
Marcel, still glancing furtively over his shoulder towards the
tent of the Parisian Striptease, brought up the rear. "Forward!" cried Jean-Baptiste. "To the miraculous Octopus!"

And now at last they stood beneath the monster and
peered upwards through the tracery of struts and wires at
the great steel column which reared itself towards the moon.
About their feet lay a tangled complexity of gears, pinions,
cranks, and winches; above their heads the great steel arms
were like silver cobwebs stretched between the stars. The
machine was certainly Jean-Baptiste's masterpiece! Indeed
they had some difficulty at first in convincing themselves that
it was real; for they were drunk and they knew it, and the
crazy structure which towered above them possessed a sort
of sublime *improbability*, it belonged to the realm of nightmare.

"It is like a gigantic umbrella," said Lucien, when he
had stared till he was dizzy, "from which the cover has been
blown by the wind."

"Ho! You mock my machine?" demanded Jean-Baptiste
fiercely.

Nothing had been farther from their minds, said Lucien,
putting his arm round Jean-Baptiste's shoulder. It must
have cost a fortune, said Sebastien, shaking him vigorously
by the hand. It would be impertinent to compare it with
anything less than the Eiffel Tower, said Sebastien, patting
him on the back. And Jean-Baptiste, delighted by their

praise of his beloved monster, fell into his slick showman's
patter as he expatiated upon its marvels.

"Here, gentlemen, you see the engine of unbelievable
horse-power, the mighty engine which once propelled a
Tiger Tank across the shell-scarred battlefield. Yet, believe
it or not, the adjustment is so delicate that it will run for
nearly six hours on ten gallons of black-market petrol! Here
is the main driving shaft; here the reduction gear—and note
that although the contrivance is as intricate as a watch,
it is also so simple that it can be erected in forty minutes
by two men and a boy. Here we have the central pillar,
hollow and yet strong enough to support the tower of Notre
Dame. The eight arms which spring out from it are con-
trolled by an eccentric attachment which causes them to
rise and fall." He pointed to the carriage at the end of the
topmost arm, which appeared as a small black blob against
the sky, with vanes fixed to it like butterflies' wings, and
the Old Comrades, craning their necks, perceived that it
was rotating slowly in the breeze.

"Those little carriages," declared Jean-Baptiste, who became more drunk as the cold wind and the brandy-fumes
together acted as a ferment upon his mind. "Those little
carriages, when the machine is set in motion, suddenly
swoop earthward like hawks descending upon their prey,
then as suddenly tower towards heaven like rockets, spinning as they go, only to plunge down again like shooting-
stars when they reach the top of their traj- traj- trajectory!"

"Truly marvellous!" said Lucien, with a small deferential
bow towards the creator of the prodigy. "And the sensation,
no doubt, is like that of flying in an aeroplane?"

Jean-Baptiste looked hurt.

"Aviators have ridden in the machine," he said. "With
one accord they assure me that nothing they have experienced

in the air, neither in peace nor in war, can be remotely compared with it."

"Stupendous!" said Sebastien. "And would it be possible to inspect the little carriages?"

"Nothing is easier." Jean-Baptiste led them up a short flight of steps on to a platform which was fortunately surrounded by an iron rail; for they staggered and swayed and clutched each other as if they were on a cakewalk. The lowest of the carriages hung alongside this platform, and Jean-Baptiste gave it a push to bring it opposite them.

"One remarks the plush seats," he said, "the Perspex windscreens manufactured from the wreckage of crashed bombers, the adjustable hoods, and the exceptional legroom. The carriages were devised with particular attention to the requirements of loving couples."

"Indeed? How tender a thought," said Marcel, examining the seats with the air of a specialist in such things.

"Is it permissible to sit in the carriage?" asked Lucien.

"But naturally." Lucien and Sebastien climbed on board and seated themselves side by side. "It is a pity," Lucien said, "that one cannot reproduce the sensations of the machine in motion."

"Even that can be arranged."

There was a short silence while the implications of this observation sank in. Then Lucien attempted to make a protest, and indeed had raised himself half out of his seat when Jean-Baptiste waved him back imperiously.

"Did we not stand shoulder to shoulder at Verdun?" he demanded.

Lucien subsided. "We did, Jean-Baptiste, we did."

"Did we not face undismayed the advancing hordes of the invader."

"True, how true," sighed Sebastian, the tears already welling up in his eyes.

"Then *Vive La Gauloise!*" shouted Jean-Baptiste.

"*Vive La Gauloise!*" cried Lucien. "I am game for any-thing! But can you make the machine march?"

"I invented it," said Jean-Baptiste simply; and began furiously to wind a small handle at the side of the platform. "This operates a most ingenious starting motor." He turned to Marcel, who stood beside him, swaying like an aspen in the wind. "And you, my friend, will occupy the next little carriage?"

Marcel made a curious choking sound. He was trying to say that he was constitutionally allergic to heights; but his tongue could not get round the sentence, and Jean-Baptiste seemed to think that he had responded enthusiastically, for he gave him a mighty pat on the back which nearly knocked him off the platform. "Ah, my brave Marcel!" he said. "Even the same as when we stood together at Verdun." He wound the handle still faster, and suddenly there came a deep tiger's roar from the engine.

"It marches!" cried Jean-Baptiste. "The engine of un-believable horse-power which runs for six hours on ten gallons of black-market petrol. Now I will engage the gears. Marcel! As the next carriage comes opposite you, embark with celerity!"

"What? Alone?" Marcel managed to say.

Jean-Baptiste pulled down a gear-handle. There was a grinding noise, the steel arms began slowly to move, the carriage containing Lucien and Sebastien swung away from the platform.

"Quick, Marcel!" said Jean-Baptiste. "Now jump on board."

"Alone?" said Marcel again, as the carriage came opposite him.

Jean-Baptiste gave him a push.

"No, no!" cried Marcel in terror.

"Very well, I will accompany you." Marcel tumbled in; and Jean-Baptiste leapt on top of him just as the machine began to gather speed. There was a swishing sound like a long sigh; and as a rocketing pheasant towers before it falls, the little carriage shot up towards heaven.

At first the sensation was by no means unpleasant. The earthward plunge of the carriage was certainly alarming, but Marcel got used to it, and the upward rush through the cold night air filled him with an unwonted exhilaration. He even dared to peer down over the side of the carriage at the dark fairground and the sleeping town beyond. There was not a pinpoint of light anywhere, not a glimmer from the long line of caravans parked round the Square, where the Parisian Stripteasers slept beside their watchful mothers; and it suddenly occurred to Marcel that this was something which perhaps nobody had ever experienced before, to swing sixty feet up through the moonlit sky above the houses where duller and soberer citizens lay abed. "What fine brave fellows we are indeed," thought Marcel, "and what a tale this will be to tell to the new blonde with the tip-tilted nose who works in the lingerie department!" He leaned back in the comfortable plush seat, and regretted that the blonde was not sitting beside him now. He glanced sideways at Jean-Baptiste's swarthy face and smiled. The smile, however, was not returned, and he was somewhat surprised at Jean-Baptiste's expression, in which there was neither pride nor exhilaration, but deep thoughtfulness.

"A magnificent machine!" shouted Marcel; although there was no need to shout, for the steady pulse of the engine could be heard only faintly and the rush of the air past the carriage made surprisingly little sound.

Nevertheless it seemed that Jean-Baptiste had not heard him.

"I said, a magnificent machine!" shouted Marcel again.

"Yes, yes, magnificent," said Jean-Baptiste abstractedly.

"And the carriages, as you said, are admirably adapted for loving couples."

"Yes. Quite."

"And the engine is surely of exceptional power."

"Yes."

"By the way, how do you stop it?"

"That," said Jean-Baptiste thoughtfully, "is exactly what I am wondering myself."

From the carriage in front of theirs, Lucien looked down as Marcel had done at the chimneys of the Hotel Lion d'Or, at the striped tops of the tents, and at the tracks of the vehicles criss-crossing the fairground.

"I cannot see him on the platform," he said.

"No doubt he is attending to the engine," said Sebastien.

"I cannot see him beside the engine either."

"It is strange. I suppose Jean-Baptiste wouldn't——?"

"Play a trick like that on his old comrades? A thousand times no!"

"Nevertheless he has an odd sense of humour. Do you remember——?"

"Yes. That story about the wheel," said Lucien, "And the man stuck on top of it. He thought it was very funny."

"It was your fault," said Jean-Baptiste bitterly. "You hesitated to embark alone. I, without a thought, jumped in beside you."

"You were drunk."

"What of it? We were all drunk. My stomach feels like a milk-churn."

"Mine also. But perhaps the engine will stop of its own accord?"

"The engine is very reliable," said Jean-Baptiste hollowly.

A long silence fell between them. Marcel tried shutting his eyes, but immediately he did so he had the sensation of falling backwards into a bottomless abyss. Opening them hurriedly, he found the moon and the stars rapidly revolving about him, and attempted to fix his gaze upon the little carriage in front which plunged earthwards and climbed skywards, plunged and climbed again, always exactly fifty feet ahead, the quarry in a pursuit that never ended. As he watched it he saw first one head and then another emerge from opposite sides of the carriage. He was unable to watch any longer, because it became necessary for him to hang his own head over the side.

"I can never remember," groaned Lucien, "which is centripetal and which is centrifugal force."

"The question is academic."

A faint glimmer of hope was born in Marcel's reeling mind.

"Jean-Baptiste," he cried.

There was no answer.

"Jean-Baptiste!"

The showman turned towards him a face no longer swarthy, but pale as a ghost's in the light of the moon.

"The Fat Woman, Jean-Baptiste! Surely——"

"She sleeps," said Jean-Baptiste in a voice of doom.

Compassion forbids that we continue to be spectators of the distresses of these four wretched men. It will be told often enough in the Hotel Lion d'Or, in the grocer's shop, in the lingerie department, and in the cheese factory, how the Mayor and his deputies and the showman Jean-Baptiste spent the night of the anniversary of the victory of Verdun. It may be that time which heals all things will even heal their own scarred memories, and they will meet again on the twenty-first of October, and drink the good wine of Bordeaux, and order the brandy and speak of this night as they speak of the half-forgotten battles around the fort of Vaux. It may be; but that day has not come yet.

So let us leave them, cooped pair by pair in the little carriages which alternately plunge like stooping hawks towards the earth and shoot up like spinning rockets towards the sky. The universe wheels about their heads, moon and stars revolve in terrible procession, and every thirty seconds the chimneys of the Lion d'Or appear like trees seen upon a skyline only to vanish again as the carriages swish by. Divorced it seems from the good earth itself, they are the inhabitants of planets within a planet, creatures caught up in the miniature solar system of which Jean-Baptiste so proudly boasted. The cold air blows more strongly, the clouds come up and hide the face of the moon, the first winter flurry of snow swirls down out of the north . . . Yes, indeed, there are some spectacles from which it is only decent to turn away; let us draw the curtain upon this one, for the church clock is striking and the strokes are no more than two—and the engine of unbelievable horse-power runs for nearly six hours on ten gallons of black-market petrol.

# Non Compost Mentis

*Yes, they do look a bit like graves, don't they? Each of the* mounds is six feet long and four feet wide exactly. Aunt Effie told me that was the size the experts recommended. She put 'em side by side for tidiness' sake, I suppose; but don't they make a depressing view from the sitting-room window? There were twenty-five of them when I took over the property. I've levelled off twenty-one. Twenty-one and a quarter, to be precise. The next owner can damn well finish . . .

Oh. You think I ought to make a job of it before we offer the place for sale? Take that armchair, then—it was Aunt Effie's favourite—and please don't interrupt me for the next ten minutes. Then we'll see if you want me to complete the—excavations. After all, you were Aunt Effie's lawyer.

So you must have known about her little eccentricities. That's all they were, until about five years ago. How shall we describe them? An overenthusiasm for causes? And while the enthusiasm lasted, the Cause was the only thing in the world for her. You'll remember when she was a British Israelite, how she never gave us any peace about the Pyramids; and how she libelled that doctor when she was an Anti-Vaccinationist; and the trouble she got into at the rally of Mosley's Blackshirts in 1938. You were always getting her out of scrapes, I'm sure.

Do you know, when I was going through her papers last Sunday, I began to count up the various organizations she was Vice-President of. There were more than fifty! The ones that stick in my mind are the Society for Improving the Condition of the Labouring Classes, the Society for the Protection of Animals in North Africa, and the Society for the Overseas Settlement of British Women—ever since Sunday I've been wondering where and why. I doubt if Aunt Effie ever refused to join anything. She subscribed to the British Field Sports Society because she favoured traditional country pastimes, and to the League Against Cruel Sports because she was sorry for the fox. In 1945, just before the Election, she gave ten guineas to *each* of the three political parties: to the Conservatives in gratitude for Winston Churchill, to the Liberals because they seemed down and out, to the Socialists because her favourite nephew was standing as a Labour candidate. That was me.

All this was mere eccentricity, wasn't it, and rather charming too. I used to dine out on that political story. One thought of Aunt Effie's little ways as quaint and endearing until—let's see, it was in 1953—she began to go in for compost. You wouldn't think it possible to work oneself up into a state of crusading zeal about rotting vegetation; but before long, as you know, Aunt Effie was possessed by compost, she was monomaniac about compost, she was convinced

that all the physical and spiritual ills of the age were due
to the use of artificial manure, and she'd discovered the
Cause above all Causes which she'd been looking for all her
life. See those pamphlets on the table? *Good Health and
Humus; Earthworms versus Chemicals; You Are Being
Slowly Poisoned.* Aunt Effie wrote those, and had them published at her own expense. When you come to think of it,
this Cause, if you can call it one, was bound to make a
special appeal to her, because it was contrary to scientific
teaching (and she was cussedly against dogma always), it
was concerned with health (hers was beginning to worry
her), and it seemed to offer a recipe for a longer life (which
at seventy-four she felt much in need of). Above all it
held out the temptation of trying to reform the whole
world irrespective of race, nation, colour and creed, a chance
which she'd been seeking since she was twenty. She must
stop people poisoning themselves or being poisoned! When
I was Parliamentary Secretary to the Ministry of Agriculture
she wrote me about ten thousand words a week to prove
how the wicked farmers were murdering us all by putting
phosphates and potash and nitro-chalk on the land.

And as if I didn't hear enough talk in the House, she'd
lecture me for hours whenever I came down for a week-end.
I visited her quite often, for I was fond of the old lady in
a way—at least I had a kind of reluctant respect for her. I
wonder who invented the fiction that Edwardian maidens
were frail, timid, and liable to swoon at the least alarm?
That generation produced some of the toughest females in
the history of our race, not forgetting Boadicea. "I bit my
first policeman," Aunt Effie used to say, "upon my twenty-
first birthday." She was a militant Suffragette, of course; and
oddly enough, for a well-brought up young woman, and an
Honourable at that, to bite a bobby's biceps through his

serge tunic was scarcely news in 1905. Mrs. Pankhurst's girls
were always doing it; and since those female commandos
were the companions of her youth, it is not surprising that
Aunt Effie regarded *our* generation as a namby-pamby lot.
"Spiritless," she'd say. "Soft. And no wonder, when almost
everything a person eats nowadays is contaminated with those
damnable, stomach-rotting, brain-destroying chemicals . . .
For my part," she would add, "I am thankful I had the good
fortune to be born when I was and to have been brought
up on good honest muck." She was never ladylike, by our
prim modern standards. *"Muck,* my lad!" She would shake a
finger at me. "The whole trouble with the world today
is that *motor-cars don't make manure."*

Then she would start talking about the dog-carts, gigs,
traps, hansoms, broughams and carriages of her youth; but
if she sounded wistful, this was not, I assure you, due to a
sentimental feeling about horses, which creatures she had
loathed ever since her early encounters with mounted police-
men. No, she was thinking of her cabbages and onions and
cauliflowers, and the good which all those horses might
have done them! Alas, the only hoofs she ever heard nowadays were those of the milkman's pony; and though from
time to time she would dash out into the lane with a shovel
and a bucket, the pony's contribution to her vegetable-
garden was meagre indeed. For the most part she had to rely
upon her compost-heap, made of lawn-mowings, hedge-
trimmings, leaf-sweepings and what not. But one heap six
feet by four was quite inadequate for her needs; before
long she had five, all in a row, looking like those "Ancient
Barrows" which they mark in Gothic lettering on the ord-
nance map. At the head of each was a little wooden board
nailed crosswise on a peg, on which she'd inscribed a date:
*Started January 10th 1953,* and so on.

It takes a vast amount of vegetation, I'm told, to make even a small heap of compost. Aunt Effie was always complaining that she could never lay hands on enough. She went forth every day with basket and secateurs, and with that abominable Pekingese dog snuffling on the lead behind her, seeking suitable material in the lanes and hedgerows. The basket proved too small, so she took to carrying a sack; then two sacks; then three sacks, which she loaded into a rubber-tyred hand-cart.

At what point does the eccentricity of one's elderly relatives cease to be something one boasts about? For that matter, at what point does eccentricity merge into madness? I daresay even the Law has a job to decide that sometimes. Take the case of my Aunt's Pekingese. The poor asthmatic creature died of exhaustion one very hot day, and I must say it shocked me when she told me she'd put *him* on the compost-heap. And yet it was logical enough; for as she pointed out, he had to be buried somewhere.

So did the hens.

Those moping, miserable White Wyandottes, which always had featherless behinds, were dying off unaccountably when I spent a few days here in 1954. Their breast-bones were nearly through the skin; and looking back, I'm inclined to think Aunt Effie *starved them to death,* not deliberately, but because she could no longer bring herself to part with any household scraps which might conceivably be turned into compost. At the time I supposed that some disease was killing them. "That's bad luck," I remember saying to Aunt Effie, when I met her carrying two scrag-necked corpses down the garden-path. But she swung them almost jauntily, and there was a glint in her eye which I found most disturbing as she answered:

"Never mind, never mind. They'll go back where they came from."

"Where they came from?"

"Into the good ground, my lad: where you and I came from and where we'll go back to one of these days, to turn ourselves into green grass for the cows that'll give milk to the next generation. 'A man may fish with the worm that hath eat of a king, and eat of the fish that hath fed of that worm.' Remember your *Hamlet;* and *Ilkla Moor?*"

As she marched off down the path towards the compost-heaps, she glanced back over her shoulder and said:

"Feathers contain more nitrogen than anything else, they say."

I began to wonder, then, whether she was quite . . .

Yes, 1954. You had the same doubts? She wanted to leave all her money to some Anti-Chemical-Fertiliser Society? And you dissuaded her? Thank you very much.

It was that autumn she decided to grow her own corn.

She'd been troubled for a long time in case the bread she bought from the baker were made of flour ground from wheat which had been fertilised and dressed with "poisons." I had given her the address of one of those firms which supply whole-meal flour from corn grown on compost specially for the benefit of crackpots like Aunt E; but that wasn't any use. "Aha, that's what they tell you," said Aunt Effie. "That's what they advertise in the papers. But *how do we know that they are telling the truth?*"—and her sly look, almost as if she'd scored off me, gave me another moment of dismay.

"I've arranged to plough up the paddock," she said.

It is astonishing what the determination of an old lady can achieve. She hired a man with a tractor, who ploughed the four-acre field behind her house. In due course she broadcast the seed, and the following summer she harvested it personally with a billhook, thrashed it with a flail she'd bought from an antique-dealer, ground it with an ancient

quern, and set her long-suffering old maidservant, Patience,
to knead the flour into dough and bake it in a special oven
which the builder had put in for her. Patience had put up
with Aunt Effie for forty years; but at last it seemed hers
became exhausted, for the next time I visited Aunt Effie,
I found her baking the bread herself. "Patience has gone,"
she said, and I wasn't altogether surprised. The kitchen,
on that July day, was as hot as a bakery; the bread,
which Aunt Effie gave me for tea, was the colour of porridge
and the consistency of very stiff porridge. It was full of
gritty bits which stuck in my teeth. "Health-giving food
grown on uncontaminated soil," Aunt Effie smiled, "aerated
by God's creatures, the worms."

It was the soil she meant, of course, not the bread.

But the cornfield, she explained to me, demanded more
compost even than the vegetable garden had done. She was
buying sawdust now from a timber mill nearby—it rotted
excellently—and she was putting all her old newspapers
on the heaps, and her old clothes, and blankets, anything
cotton or wool, anything *organic*—nylon wasn't any good.
"I put a pair of old stockings on one of the heaps and
six months later they were still there; they don't rot, you
see."

Monomania is terrifying, isn't it? Here was Aunt Effie,
brisk, efficient, rather gay as it happened, as rational as you
and I are—on any subject other than compost; and yet
she was possessed.

Her budgerigar had just died, she told me. "Never mind,
he'll soon be pushing up the wheat-stalks."

It was then that I thought it time for you and me to have
a talk together. I called at your office, you remember, but
you'd gone home. I had to get back to London, and there
were long sittings over the Finance Bill, and in the hurly-

burly I forgot about Aunt E. until you rang me up to say
that she had died.

Well, she asked for it, didn't she? Apparently she'd just
bought a patent scythe, and although the weather was very
hot she was trying it out on the nettles round the edge of
her cornfield. More material for the compost-heaps, I suppose! She was seventy-nine, and doubtless the effort was
too much for her old heart.

Poor old lady. I couldn't help being touched that she
should have left me the house, and all her money as well;
after all, she might have left it to the Society for the Protection of Animals in North Africa. It's a pleasant old house;
and as you know, I had almost decided to settle down here
permanently.

I went so far as to make a start towards getting the
garden tidy. I couldn't get any help for love or money; so
I sweated away with a shovel and a wheelbarrow, levelling
off those heaps. It was good exercise for me—I don't get
much when the House is sitting. But I didn't enjoy it, even
at the beginning. The very sight of the mounds depressed
me; they looked as if they were just waiting for the tombstones to make the picture complete. And that dripping
shrubbery behind with its dark hollies, and more hummocks
where the herbaceous border should have been, and everywhere an autumn smell of mould and decay!

I told you there were twenty-five heaps when I started.
Goodness knows how many Aunt Effie had demolished and
carted to her field where the winter corn, by the way, is
coming up in patches, because it was broadcast instead of
being drilled. Aunt Effie had persuaded herself that wheat
from broadcast seed was somehow healthier than wheat
planted in the modern fashion. Isn't it sad how the *avant-
garde* of yesterday become the obscurantists and reactionaries

of today—if they live long enough. Ah well: one's arteries harden, I suppose. Did I tell you I wasn't altogether happy about the way the party's going? Bit too Left for me.

But about those compost-heaps. I tried to do one every afternoon. They don't look very big, but I reckon there's about ten tons of soil in each of them. It's a slow job, but I worked my way along the row steadily, beginning with the oldest, which of course are the ones which are most rotted down.

Even without the inscriptions on the boards I could almost date them by the skeletons—those White Wyandottes, you know, and Chiang Kai-shek, the Pekingese. Like a geologist dating strata by the fossils! I became quite good at comparative anatomy. In the next heap to Chiang Kai-shek's I found another skeleton, which reminded me that it was a year or so since I'd seen Sir Oswald Mosley, Aunt Effie's marmalade cat.

He was in the twenty-first compost-heap. I started on the twenty-second . . .

I wonder whether you'd like to come out and have a look? Well, I think you'll have to. You were Aunt Effie's lawyer, and you've been acting for me, and I particularly don't want to be involved in anything unpleasant. I believe I may be going to the House of Lords shortly. Keep it under your hat, though.

Come along then. It may turn out to be quite explicable and ordinary. I expect we'll be having a good laugh about it in a few minutes' time. It's just that my spade—er—exposed the toe of a nylon stocking. Nylon doesn't rot, you know. Well, yes, it looks to me as if there might be *something inside it*. And it has occurred to me that Aunt Effie didn't say, "Patience has left." She said, "Patience has gone."

# The Proof

*The two men who watched her took turn and turn about.*
Towards evening the tall scowling one came back, and the
short fat one who had yawned on the hard bench for two
or three hours got up respectfully. "Nothing has entered,"
he said. Just then a bee buzzed at the open window, and
the scowling man, whom she knew as Matthew Hopkins,
strode swiftly across the room to examine it. The other followed him, and together they watched the bee intently
until it flew away.

"Only a bumble," said the short fat man.

"Nevertheless I have known them take the form of insects," said Mr. Hopkins. He added sharply, "You have
to keep your wits about you in this business."

"Yes, sir."

"Birds and animals are more usual," Mr. Hopkins went
on. He quoted some Latin which she did not understand,
and she guessed that the short man, although he tried to

look very wise, didn't understand it either. Mr. Hopkins, however, translated for his benefit. "Owls and bats and cats are especially favoured, but insects are not unheard of, by any means. Night moths and chafers for instance. And even slugs."

"Yes, sir."

"Even slugs," repeated Mr. Hopkins darkly. "So remember to keep your eyes open always. You may go now: I will watch. Dusk is their favourite hour." He sat down on the bench and stared with his pale wild eyes towards the window.

Now at last she began to understand what they were about. At first she had been so bewildered and frightened that she thought they had tied her cross-legged to the stool as part of her punishment. Sooner or later, surely, they would let her go and she would creep back to her cottage and shut the door against the gossiping neighbours and try to forget the shame and the indignities which had been put upon her. But now she realised that this new ordeal was merely a continuation of the trial: they were waiting and watching for her Familiar Spirit, or something of the kind, to come through the window. Well, they could wait for that till Domesday; for she was no witch, and despite her weariness and her cramp and the pain of the cords which bound her so tightly she still had enough assurance and confidence left to be angry.

"You can wait till Domesday," she said aloud. But the scowling man with the pale eyes took no notice, he did not even shift his stare from the window, and her own words sounded strange in the quiet room. She bit her lip, wishing she had not spoken.

It was best, she told herself, to keep silent; for they twisted your own words against you, as she had discovered that morning when they took her before the magistrate

and accused her of things which she had never imagined
or dreamed of. She had answered with spirit, and Mr.
Hopkins had said with a conventional shrug of his shoulders: "You see, sir, how the Devil puts these pert replies
into the woman's mouth?"

"Confine your answers to yes and no," said the magistrate;
and Mr. Hopkins began to cross-examine her again.

"Were you or were you not in love with the young
man called Reuben Taylor?"

"Yes," she said at last. It was no use denying it, the
whole neighbourhood had known it. Alas, she had worn
her heart upon her sleeve!

"And did not his mother oppose the match?"

"Yes."

"And did you or did you not, on his mother's doorstep,
in the hearing of several God-fearing and respectable per-
sons put a curse upon his mother, because she would not let
you go in to see him when he lay dying?"

"It wasn't a curse! I knew he was ill, and within the
house I could hear him calling for me, and—and I was so
distressed I didn't know what I said."

Mr. Hopkins pounced on her like some swift beast:

*"So you knew he was ill?"*

"Everybody knew."

"Yes or no," said Mr. Hopkins.

"Yes."

"And then he died?" said Mr. Hopkins.

She bowed her head. It was two years ago, and the world
had been empty ever since, yet she had never cried until
now. She did not easily cry. But suddenly tears came and
she hid her face, so that she scarcely heard the things which
Mr. Hopkins was saying to the magistrate nor troubled to
deny the meaningless questions he put to her: Was she

aware that Mother Taylor's dun cow had died on the first
of March, 1644, of an unaccountable milk fever? Did she
not know that the pied cow had died on the fifteenth of
the same affliction? And the roan cow on the second of
April? "Oh, what do I care about cows!" she cried, with
all the grief and loneliness of twenty-four months lapping
about her. "The milk, sir," went on Mr. Hopkins inex-
orably, "is said to have curdled in their udders, which
thereupon mortified."

At last the magistrate said:

"I find a *prima facie* case. Mr. Hopkins, you may proceed
with your examination."

They took her then to another room in the Town Hall,
but the crowd followed and clamoured at the door so loudly
that Mr. Hopkins had to let them in; and at least a dozen
people were pressing about her when the short fat man
suddenly pinioned her arms behind her back and Mr. Hopkins lifted her skirt and pressed a pin into her thigh. She
scarcely felt the prick, for she was faint with terror and
shame. "Ho, ho, a presentable witch," said a coarse voice
in the crowd. "She bleeds, she bleeds," said somebody else,
and Mr. Hopkins let her skirt fall. "The Devil has many
artifices," he said. "It is therefore proper to decide these
matters not upon one fallible test, but upon many." He
began to make much of a small wart which she had on her
wrist, and a mole on her forearm. She could scarcely bear
the touch of his questing fingers on her skin, and she cried
out in protest:

"I have had it since childhood."

"Aye, aye," scowled Mr. Hopkins, "maybe your Master
put it as a mark upon ye, as a shepherd burns a brand upon
his sheep. We will proceed nevertheless to a further experi-
ment." It was then that they bound her to the stool in the

middle of the room, opened the window, and drove out the inquisitive crowd. The Watching began.

The light from the sinking sun now came slanting through the narrow window in a thin beam which fell between her and her watcher. Somehow it reminded her of a flaming sword, and made her think of angels, from which thought she drew comfort for a while, for surely God would not let them find her guilty of these things which she had never done? So she prayed, but silently, lest Mr. Hopkins should hear her and think she prayed to the Devil and not to God:

"Make them let me go," she said, and repeated it again and again, so that soon she almost persuaded herself that when night came they would untie the cords and allow her to scurry back to her cottage just up the lane. For a few moments her faith was so strong that she shut her eyes and actually saw herself unlatching the green door and going inside among all her friendly and familiar things, the spinning-wheel in the corner, the kettle on the hob, the brown milk-jug on the table. And Tibb would be crying for her milk, for it was past supper-time; Tibb, whose eyes grew as round and as luminous as moons in the rushlight; Tibb jumping on to her shoulder and rubbing a soft head against her face.

The thought of Tibb's purring welcome gave her comfort, for during the last two lonely years she had lavished all her pent-up love on the small black cat. At least Tibb would not shun her as the neighbours had shunned her to-day, when she was being led through the streets and had called out in vain for someone to come and testify on her behalf. They had turned away, and some of them had mocked her; inquisitive heads peering out of windows had been swiftly withdrawn. Once she had heard, or thought she had heard, a blood-chilling cry of "Burn her! Burn her!" She had never felt so alone as she did then, knowing that the only one who would have spoken for her lay in the churchyard at the top of the hill.

So now in her loneliness and misery her thoughts turned to the black cat, and behind her shut eyelids she saw Tibb playing the absurd game which they played together every evening, when she would crook her fingers in front of the light so that a shadow fell upon the wall, now of a bird with flapping wings, now of a rabbit with twitching ears. Then Tibb with arched back and hackles raised would mince before the shadows, adding to them the tantalising reflection of her own tail; to and fro, to and fro, prancing, leaping, scrabbling up the wall in pursuit of the uncatchable phantom, her lunar eyes ablaze with the weird pale light that was neither yellow nor green. And so the game went on, until both were tired and they went up the creaking stairs to bed.

Perhaps she dozed, in spite of her cramped position and the cruel cords, for surely she dreamed that she was in bed, and safe, and felt in her dreams the pressure of Tibb's small body stirring at her feet. But suddenly a queer sound, a dry crackling flutter, startled her and made her open her eyes. The beam from the window was much paler now, it was no longer like a flaming sword, but the specks of dust still danced in it and through it, as through a piece of thin gauze, she saw her watcher crouch as if he were about to spring. At the same moment a moving shadow fell across the beam, there was a swish of wings, and Mr. Hopkins leapt towards the window. His leap was all the more terrifying because she did not know the reason for it; she screamed, and then the beam was clear once more and she saw the bat for a second as it fluttered away against the

pale evening sky. Mr. Hopkins went slowly back to the
bench and resumed his watching.

She did not close her eyes again, but sat taut and upright,
straining against the cords, with all her nerves a-tingle. For
the first time she fully understood her danger. Her assurance
ebbed away from her. It was true enough that she was no
witch and possessed no Familiar Spirit—ah, but *what if
something did enter the room while they watched her?* What
if the bat had blundered in? Or even the bee?

She prayed again, but with less confidence: "Please God,
don't let anything come in." Panic came nearer with the
gathering darkness, for the beam from the window had
faded altogether and the darkness crouched in all the four
corners of the room like the blurred figure of Mr. Hopkins
crouched on his bench: like him, it waited to spring. The
smallest sound made her pounding heart beat faster—even
the ping of a mosquito, which Mr. Hopkins scowled upon
as if he suspected that even such an atomy might conceal
the Devil. Outside, the barn owl which lived in the apple-
tree half-way down the lane began his evening hunting,
and because she was still young and had sharp ears she
could hear what Mr. Hopkins couldn't—the slate-pencil
squeaking of the bats as they hawked for flies. She remembered what Mr. Hopkins had said to the short fat man who
seemed to be his assistant: "Owls and bats and cats are
especially favoured."

*And cats!* Her heart thumped again as she remembered
Tibb. By now, surely, Tibb would be hungry and crying
for her supper, stalking about the cottage and down the
garden-path, only a hundred yards away, looking for her
mistress who had never failed to feed her before. What if
Tibb——? But no, that was impossible, dogs would follow

a person—to the ends of the earth, it was said—but cats
were different, their strange unfathomable little minds were
centred upon a hearth, like lonely spinsters they worshipped
household gods. So she reasoned, and was able to calm
herself a little. Tibb would not seek her, nor in any case
know where to find her. As for the bats and the owls, they
were creatures of the sky, why should she imagine that they
might blunder into a room—and through this particular
window, of all the windows in the town?

Nothing would come in, she told herself. In the morning
they would let her go.

And then she heard the cat mewing. She didn't know
which came first—the very faint, distant mewing, or the
recollection that she had screamed when the bat's shadow
fell across the sunbeam. But as soon as she heard that tiny
cry, half-way between a mew and a chirrup, she recognised
it as the answer which Tibb always gave when she called
her, and she realised that Tibb had heard her screams.

Mr. Hopkins, motionless on the bench, made no sign;
and even when the mewing came nearer he did not stir.
Perhaps even now Tibb would fail to find her and would
go back to the cottage up the lane. She strove to quieten
her breathing, and held it until the blood surged and
thundered in her ears. When at last she was compelled to
let it go, it came in short, choking gasps, so loud that Mr.
Hopkins turned his head to stare at her.

She saw him stiffen. *"Ah,"* he said. "The Devil begins
to manifest himself."

There was a sound so slight that it might have been the
stirring of the evening wind and suddenly she saw Tibb on
the window-sill, framed against the pale square of sky. For
a second Tibb paused there, ears pricked, hackles raised,
tail curved over the arched back; and then with a little

chirrup Tibb jumped and the duck-egg-blue square was empty again, the cat was on her lap purring and rubbing its head against her, and she was tugging frantically against the cords which bit into her wrists, perhaps to stroke it, perhaps to push it away.

Mr. Hopkins did not leap this time. He rose very slowly from the bench and came towards her. Almost wearily, without triumph and without surprise, *"Probatum est,"* he said. "It is proved."

# Local Boy Makes Good

*Sitting on the fo'c's'le-head, by the last light of the sun sink-*ing behind Lundy, Amos finished her, and knew, in that moment of consummation, that she was his masterpiece. He had put ships into bottles before, and his *Cutty Sark,* which he had sold in the Red Lion for forty shillings, had taken him four years; he'd drunk her price in as many hours. But this *Talavera* had been the preoccupation of his thoughts and hands ever since 1939 when he first saw her picture in the Public Library. He had gone there to keep warm, being unemployed; but he had returned day after day to copy from an old book the rig and dimensions of the vessel in which his father as a boy had sailed round the world. Fifty days from Cardiff to Algoa Bay; twenty-eight from Algoa Bay to Lyttel-ton; seventy-four from Lyttelton to the Lizard. How many times had his father told him every detail of that voyage! So Amos's clumsy pencil scratched and scrabbled in the silent Reading Room until he had drawn the *Talavera* exactly to scale. That drawing, now almost indecypherable, had voyaged in his pocket for eleven years. It had crossed the Atlantic a dozen times (there being a use now for old broken-down seamen); it had been south to Rio and Buenos Aires, north to Murmansk, through the Mediterranean on Malta convoy, and round the Cape to Colombo and Bombay. It had got wet and smudged once, when a ship was torpedoed, and had tossed for two days in a lifeboat off the Azores. Meanwhile the little wooden model, rough-hewn as yet and without her rigging, had shared the opposite pocket of Amos's duffel-coat with his pipe and a plug of tobacco. These were the whole of his possessions when he climbed out of the lifeboat at Fayal.

The masts and spars were whittled in mid-Pacific in 1945. Thence his tanker steamed to Sydney, where a telegram told him that his wife had died, and for a space the half-finished model was neglected and forgotten, rolled up with the drawing in the corner of a macintosh sheet and stowed in one of those shapeless bundles where dwell the household goods of those who lack a hearth. When Amos returned home, however, he went to live with his sister, and it was she who "to stop him moping" set him to work once more on his toy. At her small house outside Cardiff he began to fashion the sails.

He also pottered in her garden and fed the hens and grew with pride some leeks not much thicker than pencils and some cabbages without hearts; thus discovering for the first time that idleness can be pleasant to a man who has saved fifty pounds. He began to keep his eyes open for a cottage of his own and to dream of keeping a pig. He was thinking about this pig, and meticulously sewing the reef-points into a mains'l, when his son Cec arrived out of the blue, accompanied by a girl.

Amos couldn't at first remember whether he had seen this
girl before, because all Cec's girls were almost exactly alike.
They put on a lot of lipstick in a sloppy and haphazard way,
they were pale and spiritless, and their small breasts seemed
to be pressed together by their drooping shoulders; they
rarely spoke but chewed gum and disconsolately hummed
to themselves tunes out of the films. They were the kind of
girls who spent their days playing joyless games in pin-table
galleries and their nights, perhaps, making love without
passion on desolate bomb-sites.

It turned out that this was a new one; Amos did not,
however, have much opportunity of making her acquaintance, for after a few minutes, Cec turned to her and said,
"Now you muck off, see; take a little walk down to the
end of the street," and humming "I'd Do Anything For
You," she went, with drooping shoulders, disconsolately out
of the garden-gate. Cec then said (and Amos had known
it was coming):

"Well, Dad, I'm in a bit of a jam again."

"Yes?" said Amos resignedly.

Hands in pockets, leaning against the window-sill, Cec
began to describe his jam. It was something to do with
the hire-purchase of a second-hand motor-car—a transaction
which Amos, who paid cash for all his little needs, found
difficult to understand. Cec had been unable to find the
money for his last three monthly instalments and was being
threatened with prosecution. Couldn't he, then, return the
car? He could not, because he had "sort of lent it to a chap,"
whatever that might mean. Couldn't he get it back from this
chap? No, because it had been involved in a trifling accident
and would cost thirty pounds to repair. If, on the other
hand, the thirty pounds was forthcoming it could be sold
at a handsome profit, the hire-purchase firm could be paid

off, and everybody, including Cec, would come honourably
and gainfully out of the deal.

Amos listened, only half comprehending, to the familiar
tale. Cec's troubles, like his girls, were always of the same
kind. They were never simple or straightforward troubles.
They never *quite* amounted to theft or forgery, though
there was always an uncomfortable hint of police-court pro-
ceedings in the background. Nor were they ever due to the
fault or folly of Cec, except in so far as they were in some
mysterious way to be ascribed to his own cleverness. Amos
himself, after all the wretched years, still clung to a somewhat tattered faith in the cleverness of Cec. He had been
clever as a kid; and the masters at the Approved School, after
his first bit of trouble, had said he was a clever lad who
ought to make good. Then there had been that business
about a betting telegram which Amos, who couldn't read
or write, supposed was clever in a way; but again there
had been talk of a prosecution and the bookmaker had to
be squared with twenty pounds. "If it had come off," Cec
airily observed on that occasion, "I should have been a
wealthy man." Wealth, and in a strange way honour too,
were always just round the corner when Cec was in trouble.
And now, as usual, honour could be restored and profit
could be gained for a mere matter of thirty pounds or so . . .

"*Ectually,*" said Cec, with his hands thrust so deep into
his pockets that the padded shoulders of his double-breasted
jacket were pushed up to make him look like a hunchback,
"ectually, Dad, it's thirty-three quid fifteen"

Amos did not at first answer. His little toy ship lay on
the table before him, and he went on sewing the reef-points
into the sail. Let him stew, he said to himself, let him stew
for a bit. And he thought about his fifty pounds, and how
it was a nest-egg for a man's old age, and how one could

buy a weaner pig for a fiver; but in his heart he knew that
Cec would have that fifty pounds in the end.

Cec, however, having described his present trouble said
no more about it, but lounged about the room and seemed
to take a fleeting interest in the work Amos was doing. At
least he picked up the hull of the ship in an inquisitive
magpie fashion and remarked that it was a pretty thing.

"You and your ships in bottles." He grinned indulgently.
"What's she called?"

"*Talavera.* Seventeen hundred and ninety-six gross tons.
Your grandfather——"

"Oh, I know. You've told me often enough. Sailed round
the world."

"In a hundred and fifty-three days," said Amos.

"You could fly it now in about three."

It was clear that Cec could see no virtue in sailing round
the world in a hundred and fifty-three days; but to fly
round it in three was wonderful because you "saved time."
Cec was always full of ideas for "saving time." When he
put them into practice, they sometimes got him the sack
from the rather mysterious jobs which he took now and
then.

"—Saving," said Cec, after making a brief calculation,
"twenty-one weeks and six days!"

Amos, in his simplicity, dared to wonder what was the
point of saving time when you were then faced with an
almost insoluble problem of how to use it up: of "killing"
it, in Cec's customary phrase. "What have you been doing?"
his mother used to ask him when he came in late for dinner.
"Oh, hanging about just to kill time." Even at the age of
sixteen he had found it necessary to kill time. For that
reason, and not because he enjoyed the films, he went four
times a week to the cinema; for that reason, and not because

he liked beer and company, he loafed about in the pubs; for that reason, it seemed, he took up with those queer girls. "Oh, they help to kill time," he would say.

And now suddenly the latest of these girls returned from her walk. The front door banged and she came humming into the room, this co-assassin of Cec's hours and minutes. She was an automatic thing. Cec had told her to go for a little walk to the end of the street and she had done so. She said nothing, but stood and drooped and glanced about her without interest. Her jaw moved automatically, chewing gum.

Cec said with a sort of affectation of briskness:

"Well, Dad, what about our bit of business?"

Then Amos knew that there could and would be no further discussion. He couldn't, in any case, argue with Cec in front of the girl; and in a curious way he was glad, because those long disputes with Cec made him so tired. When he was younger he used to reason with the boy, and try to persuade him to learn a trade, or go to sea: "The sea, now, that'd make a man of you." And then he would lose his temper and swear at Cec and damn his eyes, and on one horrible occasion he had hit him hard with the flat of his hand across his pale face. But the result was always the same; he paid up in the end, and though he would be ashamed to admit it to himself he knew why he paid. It was simply because, despite everything, he loved this creature. Unreasonably, absurdly, ashamedly; and when Cec went out through the garden-gate and walked away with that girl, Amos would feel quite alone.

So he put down the sail he was sewing, and got up from the table, and said:

"I'll go and get it."

When he came back he sensed immediately an altogether

different atmosphere in the room. Even the girl had brightened, and she spoke once or twice, though in a very small, tired voice, addressing Cec as "Sizzle." Cec's manner now had a strange, feverish jocularity. He made nervous jokes and laughed loudly at them; and he pretended to a sudden interest in the model of the *Talavera*, taking it to the window and holding it up to the light.

"You give yourself too much trouble, Dad, over these things. Then, too much detail in 'em. They'd look just as good if they wasn't so fiddly. These bits, now——"

"Davits," said Amos. "Her boats'll hang from them."

"Well, they could be all carved out of the same piece as the hull, like, boats and davits and all. They'd *look* just the same, when you'd painted 'em. Save time!"

Amos knew it would be no good explaining, but he tried:

"The davits aren't part of the hull. They're part of the rigging. The boats hang from them in the falls. I'll make little blocks and tackle, see, so's she could lower her boats away . . ."

"She won't need to lower her boats away, not when you've got her in a bottle," laughed Cec. "Still, I s'pose it kills time," he added tolerantly. "'Spect you find it dull-like, with nothing to do all day."

He prepared to go. Taking his girl by her thin arm just above the elbow, he propelled her towards the door; like a sort of animated doll she moved obediently. They went out and Amos followed them. At the garden-gate he handed Cec the money in an envelope and Cec said briefly, "Thenks, Dad. I'll be seeing you." The girl shook Amos's hand; but she didn't say anything unless a momentary convulsion of her jaw-muscles as she chewed could be taken as a farewell. The pair went off down the street, and Amos watched the girl's weak ankles turning over at every pace because

of her very high heels; he heard her say, "Sizzle, let's go
to the flicks."

As they passed out of sight he knew the expected loneliness, and he leaned on the gate for quite a long time, thinking. It was rather a relief when at last he made his decision
to go back to sea. He had only seventeen pounds left, and
his old-age pension; and because he remembered those
days of the dole and the Means Test, he was desperately
afraid of being poor. The cottage and the weaner pig faded
out of his dreams as he stumped back into the house and
began to bundle up his belongings. Right in the middle
of the bundle, for safety's sake, he stowed the hull of the
*Talavera,* wrapped up neatly with her masts and half-finished sails, with the spools of silk which would be her running rigging, and the precious smudged drawing he'd made
so long ago in the Public Library.

And now at last she was finished! Her spread canvas as
white and lovely as gulls' wings in the setting sun, she
rode on an even keel within the clear glass bottle which
would confine her for as long as she lasted—for years and
years, maybe for a century, thought Amos in the full pride
and glory of creation; there were ships in bottles much older
than that. Gazing at her, he knew that he would never make
another model. There would be no point in doing so, because he could never make one better than this.

It had taken him the whole of his last voyage to put the
finishing touches to her. The eight-thousand-ton tramp had
had boiler-trouble on the outward trip and had tied up
at Port-of-Spain in Trinidad for a month while she was
being repaired. By the time she was patched up, and had
discharged her cargo at Caracas and taken on another at
Pernambuco, nearly five months had gone by. Aware that

there was no hurry, and having unlike Cec no ambition to "save" the fleeting minutes in order that he might squander them later, Amos spent his leisure fiddling with the sails and rigging of his toy, sandpapering, polishing, making sure that every tiny block ran smoothly; he gave the hull no less than four coats of paint and meticulously varnished and revarnished every mast, spar and yard. At last, within sight of the coast of England—it seemed a fit and proper culmination of the long voyage—he slipped the model through the narrow neck of the bottle, a moment almost as anxious as a real launching, and then went up to the bridge to do his trick at the wheel. When he came off watch the glue had set firmly and there was nothing more to do but to pull tight and make fast the silken threads that raised the masts and sails. This was a matter of minutes only; and it somehow astonished him that the moment of creation should be so brief, the preparation for it so long. "Thus the heavens and the earth were finished, and all the host of them."

So now, as Morte Point fell away on the starboard quarter, and the white surf of Woolacoombe Bay, he held up the ship against the sunset and the soft yellow light shining through her sails and glinting on her fresh paint made her come wonderfully alive, she was a ship of faery, magical, unearthly, flying before an imperceptible wind. It occurred to Amos that some watcher on Morte Point or Hartland might have seen the real *Talavera* thus as she came winging up the Channel on that evening long ago; the sunset glowing behind her canvas, the strong, steady sou'-wester in her t'gallants'ls, the crisp white foam dancing beneath her bow, her wake dying away behind her as it had died away, hissing and subsiding, right round the great globe of the world!

And her crew, with Amos's father among them, crowding

the rails, murmurous and excited, seeing England for the
first time in a hundred and fifty days, cheering the landmarks as one by one they came into view: there's Baggy
Point, there's Ilfracombe, hurray, from the crow's nest a
look-out waves an arm towards Mumbles Head and old
Swansea Bay on the port bow! How well Amos knew that
murmurous animation, that buzzing and reawakening, that
sense of seeing old familiar things for the first time, which
only sailors home from the sea can feel. How many times
in his long life, he wondered, had he run up on deck and
rushed to the rail to catch that first precious glimpse of
England? Three-score? Eighty? It might be even a hundred.

Then suddenly Amos, who had been thinking of the men
of the deck of the *Talavera*, realised that *he* was coming
home at this moment and that the landmarks awakened no
wonder, no sense of anticipation at all. His mood of exalta-
tion fell away from him. There was no home. There was
only his sister's house (and for all he knew she might by
now have let his room to a lodger) ; there was the hostel in
the docks; and there was the Red Lion. There was also a
vague gnawing apprehension lest Cec might have got into
some deeper trouble while he had been away.

He laid down the ship beside him on the fo'c's'le-head
and was no longer conscious of her loveliness, was only
aware that she had filled his thoughts for so long and was
now no longer there; she was done, she had gone, she had
sailed out of his mind and had left a vacuum behind her.
He paid now the penalty which all who create must pay:
he felt curiously empty, deflated, his spirit drained away.
And he had no sense of homecoming when he saw the cranes
of Barry and knew that Cardiff lay beyond the headland,
only three and a half hours' steaming away.

Amos did not go ashore until next morning; and Bute Street in the morning wears a blear-eyed and desolate look. A Chinaman yawns outside his empty café; coal-trimmers after a night shift trudge homewards with the whites of their eyes staring out of blackened, expressionless faces; girls who might look pretty in the evening come out haggardly from sombre tenements, fetching in the milk-bottles, coughing over first cigarettes; Lascars with the infinite weariness of Lascars slope along on their way to join their ships; and a few sailors with bundles walk the opposite way, coming ashore. Only to these few does Bute Street in the morning appear, miraculously, to be a delectable place; because it offers the first pavements, the first houses, the first cafés, the first pubs, a foretaste of hearth and home.

Amos, who had nowhere to go, was nevertheless aware of the indefinably pleasant sensation which dry land gives to those whose feet for months have felt only a moving deck beneath them. Savouring this pleasure, he walked as far as the end of the street, where he found a café open and ate a fresh bread roll—this is generally the first indulgence of men who come off ships which lack a bakery. He sat in the café for a long time, trying to pluck up courage to go and find out if his sister had taken a lodger; but at last, realising that the pubs were now open, he made his way to the Red Lion.

He knew the old barmaid there and she gave him a welcome, which is another thing sailors hanker after when they come ashore. He leaned with his elbows on the counter (one more queer little pleasure renewed) and bought her a drink. Soon some customers came in, and it was not surprising that three of them should turn out to be old friends of his, for Amos had been using the Red Lion, whenever he was ashore, for nearly forty years. To these, after a few beers, he showed his *Talavera,* unwrapping the whole of his bundle of clothes, towels and oddments to find her where she lay at the secret heart of it. She was duly admired, and the landlord recollected the model of the *Cutty Sark* and how Amos had sold her for forty shillings.

"You'd get twice as much for this one," he said. "If you could find a Yank, and he was a bit tight, you'd maybe get a fiver."

"I wouldn't sell her," said Amos almost fiercely, "for anything in the world." The landlord smiled, thinking no doubt that it would be a different tale one night when Amos had spent all his money and wanted a few more drinks.

And now there came in a man older than Amos, a fireman off a collier just back from Gibraltar, who knew all the tricks by which ships were put into bottles and who asked an expert's questions, nodding approval over the *Talavera* as she lay on the counter among the pints of beer.

"No longer such beautiful things can they make at all," said this old sailor. "A lost art it iss, man, like thatching iss in the countryside. The patience they do lack for it."

"True enough," said Amos. "Off and on, she took me eleven years."

"Eleven years! But a thing of beauty she iss, man, and worth the labour. They do not understand today. A godless age. Quick results they do demand. *You* know that well."

It crossed Amos's mind that the man was thinking of Cec, for most of the Lion's customers knew about him. Indeed, it had been in this bar, seven years ago, that a well-meaning fellow had taken Amos aside and whispered to him, "Trouble there is at home." That was the trouble which led to the Approved School. Ever since, Amos had been a little afraid when he returned to the Lion after a long voyage: afraid of the sympathetic glance, the kindly hand on the shoulder, the old friend beckoning him into a corner. However, the fireman said no more, and none of Amos's other acquaintances mentioned Cec at all. They drifted away one by one, and Amos himself was preparing to leave when the barmaid leaned over the counter and whispered:

"That boy of yours. You've been away a long time——"

"Yes?" said Amos sharply. It was a cry as much as a question. He thought he knew what was coming. Some fresh trouble; some confused, complex, incomprehensible misfortune; or perhaps after all Cec hadn't been able to square up that business of the hire-purchase car. Perhaps it was worse than ever this time—a case in the courts, even prison.

"Tell me," said Amos with a dry mouth.

The barmaid's hand, rough and wrinkled from years of washing up, lay upon his sleeve.

"But he's doing well," she said gently. "I thought you'd like to know."

"Doing *well?*"

"Some little business he has. Quite well-to-do he is getting! I saw the advertisement in last night's *Echo*. Wait a minute: I'll find it for you."

She bustled away, and Amos discovered that he was sweating, so powerful was the sense of reprieve and release. Cec doing well! Still he could hardly credit it. Yet he'd always believed, hadn't he, that the boy was clever? And hadn't the Headmaster of the Approved School written "ought to do well" on his report? "If only he will take himself in hand, he ought to do well."

The barmaid came back with the paper. She had folded it open at the advertisement page.

"There," she said. "SITUATIONS VACANT. At the bottom of the column."

Amos read:

"GIRLS WANTED FOR CLEAN LIGHT WORK IN SMALL
FACTORY. GOOD WAGES. NO SATURDAYS."

There followed Cec's name and an address.

"His own boss he is, you notice," said the barmaid. "Soon he'll be too grand to know us."

"I must go and see him," said Amos, suddenly making the decision.

"Of course. You can get there easily on the tram." Pleased with herself because she had given him good news, the old woman grinned mischievously.

" 'Girls Wanted,' I said to myself when I read it. 'Now that's just like him, that is!' I said. But they settles down in the end," she added. "Even the wildest ones, very often, they settles down and makes good."

The "small factory," from the outside, was certainly unimpressive. It consisted of a patched-up building on a bomb-site with a long jerry-built shed at the end of it. The yard was full of rubble and broken bricks. Nevertheless there was a new green gate at the entrance and a notice-board freshly painted in bold yellow lettering:

TWENTIETH CENTURY NOVELTIES, LIMITED

with Cec's name underneath, and then *Managing Director*. Clutching his bundle in one hand and his *Talavera* in the other, Amos stood before this notice. It was in his mind that so splendid and marvellous an event as the vindication of Cec required a splendid gesture on his part to match it. He would therefore make him a present of the *Talavera*.

She might not be exactly the sort of gift which would take Cec's fancy; but there was eleven years' loving labour in her and she was in fact the only important property which Amos possessed. Moreover, he reflected, if Cec was really going to settle down, as the barmaid had predicted, he would perhaps one day have a home of his own; he would marry —a nice steady girl, Amos hoped, instead of one of those sloppy ones. If so, how imposing the *Talavera* would look on the mantelpiece on Cec's hearth; and with what pride would Cec point her out to his guests, business-people perhaps, quite well-to-do and respectable . . .

"Pretty thing, ain't she? My Dad made her. *Ectually,* my Grand-dad sailed round the world in the *Talavera,* in one hundred and fifty-three days."

Perhaps Amos would never have indulged in so fantastic a daydream as this unless he had been slightly tipsy. He had had six pints of beer in the Red Lion—his first drinks for five months. They, and the barmaid's good tidings, and the ride in the rocking, bumping tram, had combined to give Amos a feeling of uplift and exhilaration which was, let us say, about half-way between drunkenness and sobriety. In this mood he was capable of such flights of fancy as were necessary to picture Cec as a family man, Cec in the company of "respectable" people, Cec (who had once pawned his only spare pair of shoes) rejoicing in the ownership of a semi-detached house . . .

Some momentary doubts assailed him when he remembered the pawning of the shoes and also the pawning of an overcoat which, it had turned out, was not exactly Cec's own property but had been "sort of borrowed from a chap." He put these unworthy thoughts away. Cec had reformed; Cec had turned over a new leaf. He was the Managing Director of Twentieth Century Novelties, Limited, and that sounded to Amos like a very important position indeed.

He went through the green gate into the yard and found a door marked *Registered Office*. Before he knocked at it he had an afterthought and hid the *Talavera* in his bundle of clothes; for he felt a sudden diffidence at appearing before Cec with the gift in his hand and decided it would be more fitting to produce it casually after he had been shown round the factory.

Nobody answered his knocking, so he went in; and like a wind dying away in the tops'ls of his spirit he felt his exhilaration go. The room was dingy and bare; there was a kitchen table which served as a desk, with a portable typewriter on it; and before this typewriter, on the only chair, sat the sloppy-looking girl, chewing gum.

It was apparent that she did not recognise him. For a few moments she went on tapping at the typewriter with two fingers. Then she looked up and said, "Yeah?"

"I just called," said Amos, "to see my son."

She remembered him now, for she gave an exclamation which sounded like "Ow!" and, becoming suddenly ladylike, stood up and extended her hand. Then, as suddenly, she withdrew it, remarking, "Wet nail-varnish. Pardon. I'll fetch Sizzle." She went out through a side door and Amos noticed once again the high heels and the stockings which wrinkled above the ankles when they turned over at each step.

He lit his pipe and waited nervously. It seemed a very long time before the girl came back, with Cec following her. Cec looked different, somehow, and the difference was nothing to do with his new grey pin-striped suit and his American tie which had a picture of a naked woman on it. The change had happened inside him and Amos, forgetting that in recent years he had only known his son as a supplicant and a scrounger, felt almost as if he was meeting a stranger. For one thing, Cec slapped him on the shoulder,

which he had never done before; and as he did so he exclaimed with a tremendous and rather terrifying jocularity:

"Well, if it ain't old Barnacle Bill back from the sea!
How are you making out, Dad?" Amos was glad he had hidden the little ship. He could not, at this moment, have
brought himself to give it to Cec; he would have felt a fool.
It would have been like giving it to someone he had never
seen in his life before.

Meanwhile the girl had returned to her seat before the
typewriter; and Cec, with his hands in his pockets, strode
up and down the small room.

"Got those invoices done?" said Cec suddenly in a stac-
cato and curiously artificial tone.

"Yes, Boss." The girl picked up his manner like a child
catching a ball.

"Cashed up?"

"Yeah."

"Let's see."

She got up and handed him a bank paying-in book with
a lot of pound notes in it. Amos, as he stood and watched,
was aware once again of the sharp sense of estrangement.
Cec had become somehow larger than life, unreal, unnatural. Amos didn't go to the pictures, or he would have
recognized the amateurish imitation of the behaviour of a
tough business-man in an American film.

Looking up from the paying-in book, Cec said with a
grin:

"Hundred and twenty smackers last week. This week we
shall knock it up to a hundred and fifty."

"I heard in the Red Lion—" Amos began.

"The little old Red Lion," put in Cec patronisingly.

"—How well you were doing. I'm glad, Cec."

"Yes, we're doing well, ain't we?" said Cec, handing back

the paying-in book to the girl and giving her at the same
time a friendly and intimate slap on the bottom. "Doing
fine. And I owe it all to you, Dad!"

"All to me?" Amos remembered the thirty-three pounds
fifteen, and the twenty pounds to square the bookie, and
the fiver to get the borrowed overcoat out of pawn; and
he was suddenly touched.

"It was nothing," he said.

"Believe me, it was everything." Cec put his arm round
Amos's shoulders. "Come along with me. I'll show you."

He led the way down a covered passage between the
blitzed building and the long shed. There was a door at
the other end, and Cec said "You'll have to put that pipe
out now, Dad. No smoking, because of the paint and var-
nish." Amos obediently knocked out his pipe, and Cec
ushered him in.

There was a wooden bench running down the middle of
the shed, at which under bright electric lights about a
dozen girls were working. Amos did not, at first, understand
what they were doing; the whole of his attention was taken
up by the girls, who seemed to be almost exactly alike. A
moment later he realised that this was an illusion; for in
fact some were tall and some were short, some dark and
some blondes. The illusion, he now realised, was caused by
the fact that despite these differences all the girls were of
the same type: they were Cec's type. They were the sort
of girls he had giggled with at street-corners ever since he
was fifteen; and there were twelve of them all brought
together under one roof! It was terrifying; it was like a
nightmare.

Cec prodded him jocularly in the ribs.

"At your age, Pop! Now then, take your eyes off 'em."
Some of the girls giggled.

"I'll show you something that ought to be more in your line," said Cec. "Take a look at this."

He went towards the bench; and for the first time Amos saw what the girls were doing.

*They were putting model ships into bottles.*

But these were not ships as Amos knew ships. They were not built; they were manufactured. There lay in the middle of the bench a pile of hulls, haphazardly heaped together, shining and glistening with the sort of paint which is used for the uniforms of lead soldiers. Now and then a girl would pick up one of these hulls and with a few deft strokes of a paint-brush suggest the hatches and the planking-in of the decks; then she would toss it casually on to another pile.

"We mould 'em," said Cec proudly, following Amos's glance, "out of papier-mâché."

Two more girls were cutting sails from what looked like a kind of celluloid material and gluing them on to the masts; others were tying pieces of white cotton to the mast-heads; and at the far end of the bench a girl apparently more skilled than the rest was inserting the finished ships in the bottles. For this purpose she was equipped with an ordinary buttonhook and a long-handled brush. As the bottle lay on the bench before her, with one hand she used the buttonhook to raise the ship's masts, with the other she applied a dab of gum to the base of each.

"Come and see the finished job," said Cec. As he conducted Amos along the line of girls he patted each in a proprietary way between the shoulders. "How are you doing, Maisie? Everything O.K., Doreen?" In an aside to Amos he explained, "No formality here, Pop. No trade-union rules. We gets on with the job.

"And now," he added as they reached the end of the bench and the last girl of all, who was putting corks in the bottles and sealing them with red sealing-wax, "Now I'll show you the genu*ine* completed article, as sold for two guineas apiece in half the pubs of Cardiff, Swansea, Llanelly, and Bristol *and* on the beach at Coney Island where the trippers go. The genu*ine* Bedou*ine* original ship-in-a-bottle which took old Barnacle Bill six months to make with his poor old horny hands!"

He leaned over the girl and picked up one of the finished jobs. As he held it up in front of Amos's bewildered eyes, a further beastliness became apparent. The inside of the bottle had been *tinted:* green for the sea, blue for the sky, white waves in between. Against this gaudy background perched the outrageous model, a painted ship upon a painted ocean. But is was a ship only in name; it bore as much resemblance to a ship as a stuffed bird in a glass-case bears to the winged creature with the throbbing throat. Amos recoiled before it.

Meanwhile Cec was saying:

"*Ectually,* Pop, the gross cost including labour is precisely fifteen and a tanner, so that gives us a hundred per cent clear when the retailer's had his rake-off. Not bad, eh? And you must admit she's a neat job, even though she *is* mass produced and she ain't got the frills that yours have. After all, Pop, you've got to keep pace with the world. Take her in your hands and have a good dekko, and tell me straight if you can see anything *wrong.*"

Amos took it, simply because otherwise it would have fallen to the floor; but he didn't want to touch it any more than he would have liked to touch one of those tarty girls. He was not a very imaginative man, nor was he gifted with overmuch sensibility; what imagination and sensibility he possessed had been spent first on Cec with his terrible, twisted cleverness and secondly on those loved children of

his hands, the *Cutty Sark* and the *Talavera*. Nevertheless,
he had enough feeling left to be aware that the prostitution
of all he believed in lay within his hands in the painted
bottle. All the cheapness and the tawdriness of the street-
corners, the whole philosophy of the pin-tables, enshrined
there!

"—And if you'll accept her, Dad, she's yours," said Cec
with a large and expansive gesture "I said I owed it all to
you, and that's a fact, cross-me-heart-an'-spit-on-the-floor.
Well, I made good in the end, didn't I, and there's a little
token to remember it by. Stick her on your mantelpiece,
Pop, and when you have your friends in of an evening——"

Amos suddenly realized that he was being gently propelled
towards the door. Cec's arm was about his shoulders, and
Cec's voice, the voice of a stranger, was loud in his ears.
In one hand he still clutched his bundle of belongings; in
the other, Cec's gift.

# The Young Capitalists

*Despite its exorbitant fees, the "tone," as Mr. Prendergast* put it, of his private school was advanced and socialistic. Not that Mr. Prendergast was Red; far from it. His socialism was of the mildest and most ladylike sort, and founded upon the teachings of William Morris. The company of rough working-men in a pub would have been abhorrent to Mr. Prendergast; but he and his staff believed firmly in wholemeal bread, the redistribution of wealth, the Simple Life, arts and crafts, folk-dancing and fresh air; they were teetotallers, non-smokers and vegetarians to a man, and moreover the school's prospectus promised that only fresh vegetables grown upon natural organic compost would be served with the boys' meals. This combination of high fees and The Simple Life (for the boys were fed mostly on lettuces) incidentally contributed to the redistribution of wealth and produced some remarkable profits. Mr. Prendergast salved his conscience by subscribing large sums to such

bodies as the Fabians, the Society for Cultural Relations
with the U.S.S.R., the Temperance League, the Anti-Vivi-
sectionists, and the League Against Cruel Sports.

There were no punishments at Prendergast's; for as the
Headmaster often said, "A Boy's Best Cane Is His Own
Conscience." A problem was therefore presented to Miss
Naylor, teacher of natural science and elementary biology,
when on the first day of the summer term she was struck
upon the forehead by a stone as smooth and round even
as David's; and discovered, hiding in the shrubbery, Tancred Major . . . "and his sling was in his hand."

She brushed aside his excuse that he had aimed not at her
but at a starling; and she confiscated the catapult, after
some heart-searching, because she entertained doubts about
the reliability of Tancred's conscience, which of course
should have persuaded him to burn it. She happened, however, to be carrying a jam-jar in which reposed a small green
caterpillar; she had dedicated this creature to the instruc-
tion of a biology class. On the spur of the moment, and to
console Tancred for the loss of his catapult, she presented
him with the jam-jar and its contents, saying as she did so:

"It may teach you, Tancred, that there is much more interest and profit to be derived from the study of a living
creature than from a poor, limp corpse; and if you keep
it long enough it will turn into a Poplar Hawk moth.
You may go."

She then went to her room and bathed her forehead
with an appropriate disinfectant. Tancred sought the company of some friends and told them of his misfortune, and
they all sang a song beginning "What shall we do with the
drunken Naylor" which happened to be popular in the
Fifth Form at that time.

Tancred was uninterested in natural science and cared
nothing for his caterpillar; but it had a curved horn upon
its tail which he thought might endow it with some commer-
cial value, and he eventually sold it to a boy called Porteous
for three sweets. He then bartered the three sweets for
fifteen inches of elastic, the square black sort, and
made himself a new catapult. You must understand that no
pocket-money was permitted at Prendergast's; Mr. Prendergast thought that its possession encouraged the acquisitive
spirit, and he had forbidden it ever since he had caught
some boys filling in football-pool coupons by means of an
arrangement with the gardener. Any cash, therefore, which
a boy might bring to the school had to be handed over to
Mrs. Prendergast, who entered the sum meticulously in an
exercise book and set it against a weekly issue of sweets.
These boiled sweets were, of course, home-made; their
wholesomeness was thus ensured. It was fortuitous that she
derived a considerable profit from them. They consisted of
monkey-nuts boiled in treacle; but to boys who lived on
lettuce, yoghurt, shredded raw carrots and wholemeal bread
they tasted much better than that.

It never occurred to Mr. Prendergast that they might be
employed as currency; but such was the case. Prendergast's
Private School was possibly ahead of the rest of the world
in that its currency was founded upon a dual standard: of
sweets and catapult-elastic. The equivalent, fixed long ago,
was one sweet to five inches. An attempt to alter it, during
a period of exceptional hunger, to 1 : 7 had been defeated
by the Prefects, whose privileges included Late Supper, in
the form of wholemeal biscuits and a glass of milk after
prep.

What are called Crazes run through all schools at the rate
of about one a term; and recent Crazes at Prendergast's had
included foreign stamps, guinea-pigs, white mice, conkers,
stilts, hamsters, and roller skates. (Catapults were endemic,
and did not constitute a Craze.) There was no particular
reason why the next Craze should have been Poplar Hawks,
for Porteous was not the kind of boy one would expect to
start a fashion. He was withdrawn, bespectacled, and pre-
ternaturally grave; his nickname was Molotov. His claim
to fame, if any, was that his father had been twice im-
prisoned as a conscientious objector and his grandmother,
having chained herself to the railings of Buckingham Palace
as a Suffragette, had subsequently died while on hunger-
strike. These facts gave him a special distinction in the eyes
of Mr. Prendergast, who saw in his grave and solemn de-
meanor the portent of yet another martyrdom in the cause
of advanced thought. Poor Molotov, however, was secretly
ashamed of his father and detested the memory of his
grandmother, who so perversely had chosen to die when
she could have afforded unlimited quantities of cream-buns.
His gravity was chiefly due to his own perpetual hunger.
Having sold his Poplar Hawk at a profit of two sweets, he
promptly went in search of some more. Miss Naylor, always
anxious to encourage a genuine interest in natural history,
obligingly showed him the poplar-tree where she had found
her caterpillar; Molotov, peering hard at each leaf through
his spectacles, was rewarded by finding five. He was lucky
enough to sell one of them to the Head Prefect; and so the
Craze began. Soon it became apparent that there were in-
sufficient caterpillars upon Miss Naylor's tree to meet the
growing demand; and in obedience to certain inexorable

laws the price began to rise. It went up to nine sweets apiece, and thenceforward the cricket pitch was deserted (for games were not compulsory at Prendergast's). The boys ranged far and wide every half-holiday, searching for the small green caterpillars with the horns on their tails. Miss Naylor observed to Mr. Prendergast, one evening after supper, that it was beautiful to watch this awakening curiosity about natural objects in the very young: "I think of 'their minds," she said, "as little flowers, so long shut, now opening eagerly to the sun."

Meanwhile it dawned upon Molotov, whose mind was burgeoning like anything, that the supply of wild caterpillars was not inexhaustible, and that when there were no more the boy who held the greatest number would be able to dictate the price. For the whole of one Sunday afternoon, during a fruitless search of the poplar-trees, he thought about this; and at last, hastening to his locker in the dormitory, he made a courageous but agonising decision. There were fifty-six sweets in the tin in his locker; for a miserly streak in his nature somewhat mitigated his greed. He counted them carefully, but he refrained from eating even one. Instead he put them in his pocket and seeking out the newest boys, the most feckless, and above all the most greedy, he displayed Mrs. Prendergast's treacle-coated monkey-nuts before their covetous eyes. That evening, driving as hard a bargain as an Irish horse-coper, he bought three caterpillars for eight sweets each; the following day he bought four. He had no more sweets, but he went to the moneylenders, three boys in the sixth form who were improving their mathematics in this way, and borrowed heavily at compound interest against Mrs. Prendergast's next issue. The ramifications of his subsequent transactions would make dull reading; they were probably no less honest that those which great tycoons indulge in as a matter of course, and it is enough to say that by half-term Molotov owned fifty-three Poplar Hawks; the price was still rising; and he decided to sell out. He did so cautiously, secretly, and in driblets, lest he flood the market and depress the price. He became rich, a little millionaire, and he tasted for the first time the delicious and corrupting power that accompanies wealth. Being unaccustomed to power, he used it tyrannically. No Prefect dared to report Molotov for leaving his clothes on the changing-room floor; for all the Prefects were in his debt. Smaller boys, some of whom owed him more than they could ever hope to pay, ran errands for him at his least behest, and even did his French preparation for him, which until then had been the burden of his days.

"One of the most remarkable phenomena of this term," beamed Mr. Prendergast in the Staff Common Room, "is the change in Porteous. He goes about with an air of positive *authority*; and what's more the boys look up to him. There are vast, untapped potentialities in that child."

"His French has improved amazingly," purred Miss Naylor, whose exposition of the lives and loves of woodlice was only part of her duties; she taught languages as well.

"His mathematics too," said Mr. Prendergast. "With his father's moral courage and his grandmother's determination, his future looks bright indeed."

Everybody, however, did not love Molotov; and the person who loved him least was perhaps Tancred, whose faulty aim with his catapult had started the whole thing. Tancred could not forget that he had possessed the first Poplar Hawk in the school and that he had sold it to Molotov for a mere three sweets, chickenfeed compared with the prices which were ruling now. He had always despised Molotov, and it was hateful to see him flourishing like the green bay tree. Tancred therefore put aside his catapult and took to searching the poplar-trees assiduously in the hope that he might discover a flock or herd of caterpillars and so do Molotov in the eye. The search, however, bored him, for his only interest was in blood-sports. He was about to abandon it for good when he found, upon the mid-rib of a half-devoured leaf, a creature so strange that it captured even his oafish attention, and putting it into his jam-jar he hurried off to see if Miss Naylor could give it a name. In shape it was more like a crustacean than a caterpillar: a "leaf-lobster," he christened it in his mind. In colour it was lime-green, the exact shade of certain desirable sweets; but it had a velvety purple saddle upon its back. Its face was like the behind of a baboon; and upon its tail it carried two scarlet threads, like wisps of cotton, which it agitated violently when Tancred teased it. However, its most amazing trick, which it performed when Tancred teased it still more cruelly, was to *spit*. It spat a small gob of what he could only suppose to be venom into his face; and when he told this to Miss Naylor she looked appropriately grave.

"Not venom, Tancred, but formic acid; it might have been quite troublesome if it had got into your eye. The creature is indeed a caterpillar, and will turn into a Puss Moth next spring. It will make a most instructive pet. The thread-like tails, by the way, are called *flagellae,* on account of their resemblance to little whips . . ."

Still bearing his jam-jar, Tancred looked for Molotov; for a pleasing revenge was beginning to take shape in his mind. He encountered him at last in the act of pulling the ear of a very small boy called Squeaker and saying, "Pay up, you little beast, or I'll *make* you squeak." The small boy, new that term, described circles about Molotov, who held him firmly by the ear. He squealed pitifully. His father, as it happened, was a noted opponent of corporal punishment, and had chosen Prendergast's because it was such a humanitarian school.

"Please let go, Molotov, please, *please!*"

"Junior boys call me Porteous."

"Please, Porteous, I'll give you my pencil-sharpener——"

"I want sweets."

"—and my special bungie with ink-eraser on one side—"

"I want sweets."

"But I haven't got any sweets. I haven't eaten any for weeks. You've had them all. *Please*, Porteous, *please* . . ."

Tancred watched this performance dispassionately; he had never seen a boy's ear pulled off and the possibility of such a spectacle attracted him. At last, however, he intervened:

"Let him go."

Molotov spun round.

"Who are you to tell me to let him go?"

"I've got a cattie in this jar."

Molotov came eagerly towards him.

*"That?* That thing? It's not a cattie; it's a bug."

"Is it now, Mr. Know-All? Well, Miss Naylor says it's one of the rarest catties in the world and it turns into a Puss Moth——"

"What's a Puss Moth?"

"Bright blue with yellow spots," improvised Tancred. "And what's more it's deadly poisonous, like a snake. Spits venom. It nearly killed *me,* but I was too quick for it."

"I say, Tancred, I'll give you three sweets for it, if you like."

"Three! I want thirty."

"Fifteen, then."

"Ha-ha. As a matter of fact, Molotov, I'm going to sell it to the Head Pre. Then we'll see what'll happen to the price of Poplar Hawks. Snooks to you."

He went off, swinging the jam-jar from its string in a way which tantalised and infuriated Molotov. He soon changed his mind, however, about selling his Puss to the Head Pre.; a better plan occurred to him, and he carried it about with him, showing it to all his friends and singing its praises to the Fifth Form, the Sixth Form, the Shell, and the Remove, even to the miserable little worms of the Junior.

"One drop of its venom, no bigger 'n a pinhead, could blind you for life; so Miss Naylor said. Turns into a blue moth with yellow spots and green eyes. The little threads coming out of its backside are called *flagellae*. That's Latin for little whips. Uses 'em on its own behind so as to whip itself into a rage. See when I poke it with a stick . . . Rarest cattie in the world, Miss Naylor said . . ."

Having thus laid the foundations of his plot, Tancred let it be known that he had found his caterpillar feeding on an oak in the spinney at the bottom of the garden. Next half-holiday, he first assured himself that almost very boy in the school was swarming up the oak-tree and then sprinted round to the poplar where he had discovered the Puss. "Where there is one," Miss Naylor had told him, "there are almost certain to be a lot more." And sure enough, before the afternoon was out, he had filled his jam-jar with Pusses. He was pretty certain, moreover, that there were none left upon the tree. Just before prep he sold the two fattest to the Head Pre., who was *ex officio* the glass of fashion and the mould of form; and from that moment Molotov's ruin was assured. The new Craze was all for Pusses, and the Prefects even promoted a competition, first

prize six sweets, for the Farthest Spitter. Prodded repeatedly
with twigs and match-sticks, the Pusses had a sad time of
it; but their miseries were nothing to those of Molotov. His
prosperity throughout had been founded upon the shifting
sands of debt. While his Poplar Hawks were worth fifteen
sweets each, he had been solvent, and the moneylenders had
left him alone; now they presented him with their bill,
calculated in compound interest, and Molotov grew pale
as he perused it. In vain he swore that he had not one
sweet left in his locker; they searched his locker, then they
searched his person, and for his last sweet, half sucked and
furred with pocket-fluff, they graciously allowed half a sweet
off their bill. He offered them all his remaining Poplar
Hawks in settlement, and they simply laughed. They tweaked
his ear until they were tired of the sport, and then they let
him go; but it was an illusory freedom, for Molotov knew
that he could never escape them for long. They winked at
him at morning chapel; they gave him significant glances
during lessons; they whispered behind his back at break;
they made the gesture of chewing sweets whenever and
wherever they encountered him. Even in the dormitory
there was no peace for Molotov; for by ill chance one of them
slept in the next bed. This boy would lie and grin at Molotov until lights went out, and then for ten minutes at least
he would chant a horrible lullaby: "We—want—sweets, we
—want—sweets" until Molotov broke down at last and cried
himself to sleep.

Thus haunted and hounded by the moneylenders, Molotov crept about wretchedly, despised by the least of those
he had tyrannised in the past. Meanwhile his mantle had
descended upon the shoulders of Tancred; and Tancred
wore the imperial purple with an air. Following Molotov's
example, he had made a corner in the Pusses, even as wicked
financiers make corners in wheat, zinc, or pepper; he waxed

rich. Bloated with sweets, he crowed, he strutted, he lorded it over all. If Molotov had been a tyrant, Tancred was Nero, Tiberius and Caligula rolled into one. He now had a collection of eleven catapults; but he no longer was interested in shooting birds with them—an eagle does not catch flies. Instead, he compelled the smallest boys, and especially Squeaker, who was the natural prey of all despots, to bend over very tight at a range of twenty yards; he then aimed his pebbles at their bottoms. On one occasion, while he was enjoying this form of target-practice, he was nearly caught by Mr. Prendergast; but he had great presence of mind and, taking a running jump at the nearest boy, he pretended he was playing leap-frog. Mr. Prendergast smiled happily to see his boys engaged in so innocent a pastime; he had been a trifle worried about Tancred ever since Miss Naylor had shown him the confiscated catapult at the beginning of term. It was a powerful, almost a lethal, weapon; and Mr. Prendergast could not forget that Tancred's father was a prominent opponent of foxhunting and other cruel sports, while his mother was on the committee of the R.S.P.C.A.

The tyranny of Tancred was unchallenged until the last Sunday of the term; and then it was Squeaker, of all people, who accomplished his downfall. This worm of worms, this least considered and most contemptible of all the measly juniors, went for a walk; and as usual wandered far afield, for he walked in search of solitude and as a means of escape from his persecutors, who were many. Thus he happened upon a poplar-tree which none of the other boys had set eyes on. It attracted his attention because it was almost entirely stripped of its leaves, and looking at it more closely he discovered that it was swarming with Pusses. His long serfdom had taught him much; he was an apt pupil of those who oppressed him. He went first to Tancred, and offered to keep his mouth shut for the trifling sum of fifty sweets.

Tancred had planned to auction his whole collection of Pusses in the dormitory that night, for he calculated that the usual end-of-term jollity would put the buyers in a liberal mood. He therefore paid the blackmailer's fee. Squeaker, pocketing his booty, ran off and told all his friends about his find, and also all the Prefects, to whom he was a notorious sucker-up. Tancred did not learn of his perfidy until he tried to auction the first caterpillar. He was then confronted with the spectacle of jam-jars waved triumphantly from every bed. "Bid for a Puss! We'll *give* you some of ours, Tancred. We've got *hundreds*. Sucks to you!"

Shortly afterwards Miss Naylor came round and put out the lights. When her footsteps in the corridor had died away, three shadowy figures rose up and, tiptoeing across the room, gathered silently and purposely about Tancred's bed. The moneylenders were on his trail.

At the station next day, as the boys crowded into the train, Tancred and Molotov sought out an empty carriage and entered it together. Their common misfortune had drawn them close; and they sat opposite each other, rather shyly, each with a jam-jar upon his knees.

"I brought my Pusses," said Tancred half apologetically at last. "Dunno why."

"And I brought the last of my Poplars," said Molotov. "I forgot to feed 'em, as a matter of fact, and most of 'em died. This one was so hungry he'd even eat lettuce. I gave him half my dinner. I say, Tancred, I bet you're glad to be going home."

"The grub's not much better," said Tancred wistfully. "My parents are vegetarians."

"So are mine! Isn't it stinking? They feed you as if you were a cattie. My Poplar's got quite *fat* on lettuce. Look."

Tancred dutifully admired it.

"My Pusses," he said, "make funny cocoons, out of chewed-up bark. Rather fun to watch 'em"

"I thought," said Tancred, "I might *go in* for natural history."

"Funny. So did I. Thought I'd rather like to be a Prof. when I grow up. Not with a beard, of course; but *Butterfly Hunting up the Amazon*—you know the sort of thing."

"*My* report," remarked Molotov shyly, "says '*Biology V.G.*' Does yours?"

"'*Biology V.G. Mathematics improved. Shows great interest in Nature.*'"

Across Molotov's sallow features there flitted the shadow of a smile.

"I say, Tancred——"

"Yes?"

"If we're both going in for bughunting—old chap—we might—er—do it together, mightn't we?"

"Jolly good idea."

Mr. Prendergast, seeing off his boys, waved to Tancred and Molotov. He was rather surprised to see them sitting together; he'd always thought they didn't get on. It struck him how much older and wiser they both looked; and indeed they did, for one cannot become as rich as Timon, and lose all, without learning a few lessons. How quickly boys grew up, thought Mr. Prendergast, under one's very eyes! How *responsible* they looked, those two, and how *serious*. But then the "tone" of his school—if he might venture to congratulate himself—the "tone" was so different from that of other schools, somehow.

"Good-bye, boys! Good-bye, Porteous! Good-bye, Tancred! Have a good hol.!" And in an access of enthusiasm for the tone of his school Mr. Prendergast pulled out his handkerchief and waved it frantically at the departing train.

# Cherry Ripe

*You would have thought there was a considerable skirmish*
going on at the bottom of the village. Old soldiers drinking
in the pub pricked up their ears and said Ha-ha! like Job's
warhorse. One of them was reminded of the sniper who
had so narrowly missed him before Arras; a sudden brisk
fusillade jogged another's memory with recollections of
the Battle of the Marne; a dull boom which sounded like
cannon set the younger men talking about Cassino and
Alamein. Even George Jenks, who is seventy-five, pulled up
his sleeve as if he were one of Henry's veterans on Saint
Crispin's Day and proudly showed the wound he had got
at Ladysmith. And meanwhile, Mr. Parker and Miss Philpotts, who owned adjacent orchards, strove passionately to
keep the birds off their cherries.

Both had a bumper crop, and both were notably avari-
cious; they grudged even the smallest tomtit his pitiful tithe.
Moreover, cherries were fetching a record price, but it would

be a week at least before theirs were ready for picking. So
all day long the noise of battle rolled—and the next day
and the next—until Mr. Parker and Miss Philpotts became
nearly worn out with their vigil. For the untiring birds were
early risers and late diners. A host of clattering jackdaws
took off from the church steeple to make the first dawn-raid
at about 4:30 A.M. and the blackbirds were still sitting over
their dessert at half past eleven in the evening. You might
have supposed, therefore, that the exhausted neighbours
would have taken turns at their sentry-go, sharing the
nineteen hours' vigil between them; but unfortunately they
could come to no such agreement, because they held completely different views about how the birds should be
frightened away.

Mr. Parker's method was to fire his ancient, rusty twelve-
bore indiscriminately into the trees. "To blazes with the
Wild Birds' Protection Act," said Mr. Parker, "why don't
the billymugginses in Parliament pass an Act to protect
my cherries?" And indeed his cherries did seem in need of
protection, not so much from the birds as from Mr. Parker.
himself; whoever ultimately ate them would surely break
his teeth on lead-pellets. Luckily for the birds, Mr. Parker's
shooting was erratic: anger and old age between them un-
steadied his aim. Now and then, however, a small soft
bundle of feathers came tumbling down with the cherries
and twigs and leaves. It might be a tit or a bullfinch or even
a spotted woodpecker, for all birds were thieves in Mr.
Parker's opinion, and if you protested against the unselective
slaughter he answered soundly with a sonorous word which
he had got out of the Encyclopædia: "What do you think
I am, a hopping Hornithologist?" The chaffinch on the
cherry's limb A blasted chaffinch was to him, and it was
nothing more.

But Miss Philpotts, who was a retired schoolteacher, was troubled by humanitarian principles. She had taught small children for fifty years that Everything Had Been Put Into the World with a Purpose, even wasps and earwigs, cockroaches and slugs. She clung bravely to this faith even when a flock of gluttonous starlings descended upon her trees; and although she possessed a gun, which had belonged to her brother, she fired it as a last resort and then only "into the air"; that is to say, "in any direction other than towards the birds." In the main, she relied on the erecting of scarecrows, on shouting at the birds in a monitory voice, on the rattling of clappers and the beating of tin-cans, and on the letting off of huge maroons which she bought from the ironmonger's. It was these which startled the village every hour or two with a deep boom like cannon.

Alas, the birds took very little notice of her devices. They perched happily on the scarecrows (which were cut out of paste-board in the likeness of tenuous, two-dimensional and improbable cats); they soon came to regard the tin-cans in the nature of gongs calling them to dinner; and the maroons, which exploded so violently that one of them burned off Miss Philpotts's eyebrows, merely caused them to flutter from one bunch of cherries to the next. Poor Miss Philpotts went distractedly between the trees, clapping her hands till they tingled and addressing the bloated flocks as if they were schoolchildren: "Now fly away, you naughty birds, you'll give yourselves tummy-aches. *Go away!*"

By mid-week the tempers of both cherry-minders had become considerably frayed—and no wonder; for they gobbled their meals so hurriedly that they gave themselves indigestion, the appalling row which they made in the orchards began to get on their nerves, and their short night's sleep was troubled by dreams in which the sky was

darkened by the sable wings of enormous fructivores. Miss
Philpotts complained that Mr. Parker's gunfire gave her a
splitting headache, and Mr. Parker discovered in Miss Philpotts's voice the likeness of an intolerable caterwauling. They
had always been bad neighbours and were both notoriously
argumentative; for Mr. Parker read popular philosophical
tracts and constituted himself a know-all whereas Miss Philpotts believed everything which she had taught to the schoolchildren during fifty years. Often they would wrangle
ill-naturedly for hours across their boundary-fence over such
subjects as the Literal Truth of the Book of Genesis. But
now that they were tired out, irritable, and moreover fully
armed, their disagreement was bound to take on a more
personal aspect, sooner or later; and it did so on the morning of their fourth day's vigil, when Miss Philpotts let off
her gun "into the air" but unfortunately canted it at an
angle which sent the pellets showering down upon Mr.
Parker's head. He marched up the boundary-fence and demanded an explanation.

"I was only shooting it in the air," said Miss Philpotts
defensively.

"That's as may be," said Mr. Parker, "but there's air all
round you, isn't there?"

Miss Philpotts admitted that this was true.

"And there's air all round me," went on Mr. Parker,
whose argumentative style bore some faint resemblance
to that of Socrates, "otherwise I'd be dead of suffocation,
wouldn't I?"

"A good job too," said Miss Philpotts unsocratically.

Mr. Parker ignored this and continued his labyrinthine
search for truth.

"So you'll agree that if you shoot 'into the air' and it
happens to be my air, you're shooting at me?"

The dialectical method was unfamiliar to Miss Philpotts;
but she was not lacking in tactical sense and she fell back
instinctively upon that last refuge and impregnable fortress
to which philosophers retire when they want to gain time
and collect their wits.

"What exactly do you mean by *your* air?" she said. "The
air's free, isn't it?"

"My air is where I am," propounded Mr. Parker; and
for nearly half an hour they continued this extraordinary
metaphysical argument, while the thrushes stripped the
cherry-twigs methodically, branch by branch.

Worn out by intellectual acrobatics, they returned at last
to their stations, but towards evening a second crisis occurred. Mr. Parker let off his gun at random into a tree near
the edge of the orchard and, by ill-chance, mortally wounded
a white bird with a yellow bill which fluttered painfully
across the boundary. Miss Philpotts happened to be standing
there beating her tin-can like a drum-major; the bird flopped
tragically at her feet and promptly died. Mr. Parker, who
had never before seen a white bird with a yellow bill,
walked across to the boundary to satisfy his curiosity, and
when he got there Miss Philpotts from behind the fence
rose up in fury before him, holding the limp body in her
hands.

"Now you *have* done it," she reproached him between
sobs of pity and rage.

"Done what?" hedged Mr. Parker.

"You've killed a white blackbird," accused Miss Philpotts.

"A what?"

"A white blackbird."

"There is no such creature," said Mr. Parker dogmatically.

"How can you stand there and say there is no such

creature, when you see the plain evidence pouring out its
life-blood before your eyes—" and she stroked out the tousled
feathers on the poor bird's immaculate breast.

"I can see no such thing. I can see a white bird," said
Mr. Parker in his maddeningly pedantic way, "but even
you can't make me believe that black is white and vice-
versa, and if it's white it can't be black and therefore it
isn't a blackbird."

"Isn't it, Mister Know-All, isn't it?" said Miss Philpotts.
"Then let me tell you that a white blackbird is a freak or
sport of nature, and a very great rarity, and this white blackbird was probably the only white blackbird for fifty miles.
And now you've killed it."

"How could I know," said Mr. Parker reasonably, "when
I let off my gun at the tree, that there was a Sport of Nature
hiding in it?"

"I'll tell you what you are," Miss Philpotts went on,
"you're not only a wicked ignorant man, you're a cruel
monster, and you're exactly like the Ancient Mariner who
shot the Albatross. Now I come to think of it you've got a
nasty glittering eye just like he had; and I shouldn't be
surprised if what you've done brings you bad luck for the
rest of your mortal life."

As she continued to stroke the dead bird's breast, a little
trickle of blood welled up and stained its whiteness. Now
Miss Philpotts had often declared that the sight of blood
made her feel faint, but the spectacle of this innocent blood,
crimson upon the snowy feathers, had a completely different
and most surprising effect, for she suddenly drew up her
dumpy figure to its full height and for all the world like a
knight of old throwing down the gauntlet she uttered her
terrible threat and ultimatum:

"Mr. Parker: I can use a gun myself as you well know and I swear to you that if you fire at the birds again *I shall shoot to kill!*"

Mr. Parker stared at her, speechless with astonishment.

"And I don't care," added Miss Philpotts between sobs, "if I hang for it."

Mr. Parker shrugged his shoulders and shambled away. Hysteria, he said to himself: it was no use arguing with a hysterical woman. "She'll soon get over it," he thought; and he noticed out of the corner of his eye that she was hurrying back towards her house, carrying the bird before her in cupped hands. "Going to bury it," hazarded Mr. Parker, "like she buries her dogs and cats with silly tombstones over their graves." And he let off both barrels at the nearest tree in a gesture of defiance. Nevertheless he was a little disquieted, a few minutes later, when he saw Miss Philpotts coming back with a purposeful look on her face and the gun under her arm. There was no knowing what a hysterical woman might do, or any woman for that matter, and already—perhaps it hadn't been an accident after all?—she had showered him with pellets. So he edged over towards the far side of the orchard, and just to show that he didn't intend to be intimidated aimed his gun ostentatiously at a tree. Then he remembered a man he'd read about who had lost one of his eyes through being hit by a shot-gun pellet at more than a hundred yards, and he decided not to shoot. It was dusk already, and most of the birds had gone to roost. No doubt by to-morrow the absurd woman would have got over her tantrums.

But at dawn next day, when Mr. Parker returned to his orchard, Miss Philpotts was already on guard with her gun. He gave the boundary a wide berth, and took up his position against the far hedge, which the jackdaws usually crossed

on their way from the church steeple to the cherry-trees. As
he did so, Miss Philpotts moved in what he was bound to
admit was a rather menacing way towards the boundary-
fence.

The jackdaws arrived with their usual infuriating clatter,
and Mr. Parker lifted his gun. So did Miss Philpotts. He
stepped behind a tree and put his gun to his shoulder again,
but Miss Philpotts swiftly changed her position as if to cover
him. Mr. Parker lowered his gun, and Miss Philpotts lowered
hers.

At noon the old soldiers in the pub remarked on the unusual quietude. There hadn't been a single gun-shot all
morning. No clappers, no tin-cans, no maroons. It reminded
them, they said, of the queer unnatural hush before the
barrage which began the great Easter offensive of 1917.

And down in the orchards, like chessmen moving from
square to square in an interminable game, Mr. Parker and
Miss Philpotts alternately took six paces to the left or to
the right, raised their guns, lowered their guns, took six
more paces, raised their guns, lowered their guns, in grim
and deathly silence, while over their heads in the leafy
boughs the glutted jackdaws pecked the berries in play
and a host of smale fowlës made melodye.

# Elehog

*When I found the cardboard box with holes in its lid* awaiting me on the hall table I took the usual precaution of holding it up to my ear; for in this way it is possible to make a rough-and-ready diagnosis of the contents of such boxes with which kindly neighbours humour the whim of amateur naturalists. If there is a scrabbling of little feet I expect to find a lizard, a bat, a field-mouse, or a mole trying to dig his way through the bottom of the box with an action like the breast-stroke of a strong swimmer. If there is a buzz, or a frantic drumming of wings, I take care to shut the windows before I look inside the box; for the captive will probably turn out to be a butterfly, a hawk moth, a cock-chafer, one of those big dragon-flies which look like dive-bombers, or even an infuriated hornet.

On this occasion, however, there was no sound at all; neither feet nor wings nor squeak nor chirrup; and that meant, in my experience, either that the prisoner was a caterpillar or that it was moribund; a shrew, perhaps, chewed by a cat, a nestling fallen out of a tree, or a leveret partially decapitated by a scythe. I opened the box in the gloomy anticipation that I should have to put something out of its misery.

But as it turned out the little beast inside it looked far from miserable; he was without exception the most contented little beast I had ever seen. He had made himself, already, a neat and cosy nest out of the mosses and ferns which his captors had thoughtfully provided, and he lay there sleeping, curled nose-to-tail. When the light fell upon him, he stirred slightly and yawned. He was a very small hedgehog, so young that his prickles were not yet prickly, but were no stiffer than coarse hair.

The first thing to do, when little beasts arrive in cardboard boxes, is to feed them; so I put some milk in a fountain-pen filler and held it adjacent to the baby hedgehog's nose. His response to this trifling kindness endeared him to me immediately. Without opening his eyes, he widely opened his mouth; and without troubling to move his body, which was arranged so comfortably in the improvised nest, he sucked and sucked until the fountain-pen-filler was dry. Then he licked his nose with a pink tongue, closed his mouth, and resumed his slumbers.

This trustful acceptance of fate, this attitude of "open your mouth and shut your eyes and see what the good Lord sends you," this touching confidence that the world had nothing but good in store for him, was characteristic of the small urchin throughout his short life. When he grew too big for the box, he lived for a time among a pile of old clothes which we had arranged for him in a corner of our sitting-room. Accepting without question this bigger and better bed as a gift from the kindly providence, he straight-

away made a new nest and promptly went to sleep in it.
We placed a saucer of milk in the fireplace at the other
end of the room, and two or three times a day for our
own amusement or for the entertainment of visitors we
removed the hedgehog from his nest and carried him across
to the saucer. He never bothered to open his eyes to see
what was in it. If it had contained hemlock or arsenic he
would trustfully have lapped it up. When he had drunk
the lot, he turned round, opened his eyes at last, and wad-
dled slowly back to his nest. He had discovered, while only
a few weeks old, the secret of perfect happiness. He feared
nothing and questioned nothing, desired nothing more than
he had, ate and slept, and dreamt no dreams.

His ponderous waddle, when he was on his way home full-
fed from the saucer, resembled the action of a slightly
drunken sailor: his hind quarters as he walked swayed
gently from side to side. His brief and rather fat grey tail,
and the genial appearance of his undulating backside, reminded one somewhat of a miniature elephant; and this
got him his name. He was undoubtedly a Hedge Elephant,
declared my wife; and, improving on this next day she
christened him Elehog.

Although he was far too wise ever to go out of his way
in search of anything that didn't fall into his reach like
manna from heaven, he soon became inquisitive and acquisitive about things which he happened to find in his path
during his journeys from the saucer to his nest. If they
seemed edible, he ate them; if not, he carried them home.
Thus, when he encountered in the fireplace some paraffin
firelighters, he devoured nearly half of one before we saw
what he was up to and dragged him away; and apart from
acting as a gentle purge the strange meal did him no harm.
If he met with a pair of boots he would always lick the

polish off them before proceeding on his way. As for less
edible things, he seemed to like them for their own sakes
and not for their utility, as misers love their gold; for if
he found a match-stick he would pick it up, carrying it in
his mouth like a retriever, and take it to his nest where
he kept a little pile of match-sticks, bits of string, ribbons,
cinders and scraps of paper. But, I repeat, he never deliberately sought these things; that would have been far too
much trouble; that would have been a waste of precious
eating-and-sleeping-time; that would have been incompatible
with the dignity of a small Elehog. He merely accepted
gratefully whatever the gods sent him; and he was rewarded
by a multitude of such presents, because it was fun to drop
ribbons and match-sticks into his homeward path.

It is often said that hedgehogs are excessively verminous;
but we never found any fleas on Elehog—although he would
sometimes pause in the course of his slow and dignified
walk home to scratch himself in a contemplative way with
his hind leg. Probably baby hedgehogs (like some human
babies) catch their parasites from their mothers; and Elehog's mother had disappeared soon after he was born.
Berry-picking schoolchildren had discovered him abandoned
like Moses among some rushes in a hedgeside ditch; his
mother, for all we know, may have found her way into a
gypsy's pot or been run over by a car, which is a common
accident among hedgehogs when they wander short-sightedly
and far afield in the early autumnal nights.

Anyhow, Elehog's stiffening bristles gave shelter to nothing
that jumped or crawled; and it was for quite a different
reason that he had to be banished from our sitting-room
in the end. His little messes, which were bright green, unfortunately did not match the green of the carpet; so his
nest was removed to a back room where in his easy-going

and contentful fashion he quickly settled down and began
to add quantities of raffia and garden-twine to his store
of ribbons, match-sticks, and string. We had thought of
turning him out into the garden, but he was still very small
and we were afraid lest our neighbour's dog, notoriously allergic to hedgehogs, might discover him before he had retired to a secret hibernaculum. Winter was coming on, and
he was very comfortable in the back room. We filled a
second saucer with some crisp wheat flakes, which he carried one by one into his bed and from time to time devoured them with a loud crunching sound, as if he were
cracking nuts. The first frosts, however, made him even
more slumbrous than he had been before, he woke up
only on the mildest days and made less frequent journeys
to the two saucers for a drink of milk or to collect another
wheat flake to increase his winter store. In his heap of
old shirts, surrounded by his numerous and oddly-assorted
possessions, the little capitalist dozed happily and continued
to practise his peaceful philosophy of live and let live.

Alas, it is too harsh a world for such gentle philosophers;
it is too full of roughs and toughs with hungry bellies and
long teeth. In one of the floor-boards of the back room
there was a small hole caused by dry-rot, and out of this
hole one night there crawled the swift assassin. We can only
guess what happened after that. Perhaps the rat, lithe and
silent and terrible, crept up on Elehog as he slept and slew
him as Macbeth slew Duncan; perhaps Elehog who was so
trustful and unquestioning accepted his murderer as merely
another gift of the good providence—and went forward
without fear or doubt to play a game with him. It must
surely have happened that way; for Elehog's prickles were
already stiff and sharp, and they would have provided him
with a ready defence if it had occurred to him to use them.

But he had not learned, he had never needed, to use them;
in all the three months he was with us we had never known
him to curl up, and he would allow himself to be picked
up and handled without ever troubling to raise his backward-
sloping spines.

I can imagine him waddling slowly towards the hateful
rat and sniffing it with the same friendly inquisitiveness with
which he sniffed boots and match-sticks and bits of string;
and then, I suppose, it was quickly over, for the assassin
had him by the throat. Poor little Elehog discovered too
late what pacifists wiser than he have often discovered too
late: that there is a kind of aggression which doesn't even
allow you sufficient time to turn the other cheek. You can't
reason with a rat any more than you can negotiate with a
bomb. So much for live and let live.

His slayer dragged Elehog to the hole, where we found
him in the morning, jammed halfway down it by his prickles,
gnawed and bloody, with his hind legs stiffly sprawled out,
and his absurd backside and his short, fat, elephant-grey
tail ridiculously pointing at the ceiling: nothing peaceful,
nothing comforting, nothing in the least heroic about that
ending, only the ancient grotesquerie of violent death, the
cruel parody of a lifelike attitude, which is always the sig-
nature of the roughs and toughs when they write their
sneering answer to gentle creatures who practise the philosophy of live and let live.

# Vive la Différence

*You would never have believed it of Miss Protheroe. You* would not have thought her capable of anything so decisive as the deed she did upon that Sunday morning before the village was awake. For she was such a mousy little woman: wouldn't say boo; timid and defensive in her trim thatched cottage with its garden prim as she was, and a notice on the garden-gate NO HAWKERS because she was afraid of them, whatever they might be hawking. She was also afraid of big dogs and loud motor-bikes and gypsies and destructive children and men singing on the way home from the pub and of anything in the nature of Goings On. Indeed, the only time she ever ventured to express an opinion at the Women's Institute Meeting, which she went to every Tuesday, was when she whispered, faint and chirrupy as a mouse in the grass, her disapproval of the Goings On in the new bus-shelter that had been put up opposite the Post Office. The boys and girls went there after dark and played transistor

radios and small amorous games, and tickled and squeaked
and sometimes got up to mischief which they could have
much more discreetly got up to in the woods behind the
village or on the springy, bouncy turf of Brensham Hill.
But for their own mysterious reasons they preferred the
bus-shelter, where they also chalked on the walls such state-
ments as *Billy Bradshaw goes with Sally W.* and drew hearts
pierced by Cupid's arrows. Miss Protheroe was naturally
against all this, and apprehensive of what it might lead to.

"I think we should nip it in the bud," she said; but so
quietly that Madame President had to ask her to say it again.

"I only said . . . er . . . perhaps . . . oughtn't we to nip
it in the bud?"

Because some of the women heard it twice, the phrase
stuck in their minds; and later, as you shall see, they had apt
occasion to recollect it.

Miss Protheroe's garden exactly reflected her personality.
Nothing ever rampaged in it. The flowers were polite, pastel-
coloured, faint-scented. The aromatic herbs by the back
door were kept in order, snipped and nipped if they showed
the least sign of becoming obstreperous. Upon the tiny lawn
nor daisy nor dandelion dared to show its head.

How different from the garden next door, where Mr.
Toombes had let things go so that the place was a wilderness of dark dank evergreens, and evil weeds like woody
nightshade, and once-tame flowers run wild like the boys
and girls in the bus-shelter: lax lupins, degenerate delphin-
iums, and honesty seeding itself everywhere in the shade and
scattering its seeds into Miss Protheroe's borders so that she
tut-tutted, "Honesty indeed! More like Dishonesty, if you
ask me!"

Mr. Toombes made the excuse that he never had time.

He was a funeral furnisher who worked in Cheltenham, where in those days there was a lot of death because old soldiers went to die there. The colonels and majors and captains half-kippered by curry, their livers hobnailed by chota-pegs, settled in the salubrious town and came soon into the capable hands of Mr. Toombes and were buried. He left Brensham Village each day by the earliest train and came back by the latest one. No time for gardening save at the week-end; and what could you do with a wilderness in a week-end? So he let Nature have her way in his garden; until the time of his retirement.

Then it was Miss Protheroe who urged him to tidy things up; who chirruped and whispered and breathed into his ear, oh so diffidently, her ideas of how Order might come out of Chaos. Spray the nightshade, *ruthlessly;* uproot the honesty; dig up the dandelions; lop the laurels, grub up those gloomy yews, discipline the box-bushes, trim this, trim that, let in the light at last . . .

But Mr. Toombes was by nature funereal. He liked his evergreens. He clung to them perhaps because their dull-green was perpetual. They didn't die away in a sunset blaze like a man's last hopeless passion each October; they didn't like deciduous trees, remind you how old you were when they renewed themselves with little fresh buds in the spring. The evergreens matched Mr. Toombes; and whatever good advice Miss Protheroe might whisper, he was determined to retain them. He got rid of the nightshade, dealt with the dandelions, managed even to produce a sort of shaggy semblance of a lawn, which always looked a bit mangy like the tomcats which Miss Protheroe dreaded because the terrible urgency of their caterwauling intruded into her chintzy enclave like a bull into a china-shop. But he insisted on keeping the sable cypresses, the box-bushes, and the yews among which a tawny owl hooted every night, giving Miss

Protheroe the shudders because of an old superstition that a hooting owl meant someone was going to die. Mr. Toombes had always insisted that he liked the owl; and well he might, since people dying were more or less his bread-and-butter, as you might say. But Miss Protheroe was almost as frightened of death as she was frightened of life, and she simply hated the sinister owl that dwelt in the sad, dark trees which shaded part of her garden.

"Perhaps . . . now you're retired . . . ," she breathed one morning to Mr. Toombes, "you might find time to prune them just a little? Look at that box-bush over there, all out of shape; I don't know what it reminds me of—a hideous old crow with a long beak and a besom instead of a tail!"

"I've often wondered what it was meant to be," said Mr. Toombes. "Once upon a time *somebody* must have trimmed it into the shape of *something?*"

"Of course! And the cypresses," said Miss Protheroe. "And some of your nasty old yews. Look at those two on either side of your front door—Grecian urns they must have been, before they were let grow all tufty and shaggy."

"What do they call it?" said Mr. Toombes. "Toxicology or toxophily or something?"

"No, that's poisons and archery," said Miss Protheroe, who spent a lot of her time doing crossword puzzles. "Topiary is what you mean."

"Well, I daresay topiary was all right when you could get a gardener for a shilling an hour."

"You might have a go at it yourself," said Miss Protheroe, with a faint hope that she could persuade him to trim up those trees. "You might make a start on that box-bush: see if you can trim it back into a peacock. I'm *sure* it was a peacock when my auntie lived where I do and I used to stay with her in the summer holidays."

Mr. Toombes grizzled and grumbled. Waste of time, he

said, and there was nothing like clipping to make your wrists ache, and he'd have to use a step-ladder and heights made him giddy. Nevertheless, four days later, Miss Protheroe through her parlour window heard the corncrake noise of steel on a grindstone, and then the sharp snip-snip of the shears. Hurrying out of the house, she was gratified to find that the seed she'd sown in Mr. Toombes's mind had germinated already. In his waistcoat and shirt-sleeves, three steps up a step-ladder, an old straw-hat rather jaunty on the back of his head, he was chopping off the long bits that sprouted from the hinder part of the beaky crow or whatever it was that had grown out of the box-bush.

"Dunno that I'm much of a hand at peacocks," said Mr. Toombes, very red in the face from his exertions but more cheerful than Miss Protheroe had ever seen him before; funeral furnishing already perhaps half-forgotten. "But I thought I'd make a start on the cockyollybird's backside."

Miss Protheroe, hurrying back into the cottage where she always took refuge when rough, raw life threatened to intrude upon her, could hardly believe her ears. Had Mr. Toombes, so grave, so funereal, really used to her that rather coarse expression? There was a rude joviality about "cockyollybird's backside" that was quite out of keeping with everything she had known or supposed about Mr. Toombes. Perhaps his whole character was changing in his retirement; perhaps his grave respectability had never been more than skin-deep, put on like his frock-coat and top-hat for the benefit of the forever respectable dead? How alarming if that should prove to be true! *Men,* Miss Protheroe whispered to herself darkly, *you could never be sure about Men.*

You cannot, complained Mr. Toombes, have lessons in topiary, go to Evening Classes in topiary; you've got to do it by the light of nature. And always it's a matter of trial and error; the Artist in you is your only guide.

This was the first time he had ever hinted to Miss Protheroe that he had an Artist in him, and it only increased her apprehensions, for she had heard nothing good about Artists, and much that was bad. Day after day, snip, snip, snip, Mr. Toombes practised on his peacock. He'd never had a hobby before, and perhaps that was why he took this strange hobby as severely as someone who takes measles late in life. It was like a fever with him. Sweat poured off him during the summer days: snip, snip, up on the stepladder in shirt-sleeves and straw-hat, from after breakfast until opening-time . . .

That was another alarming thing. Mr. Toombes never used to touch a drop, Miss Protheroe had always understood. Now he went twice a day to the Horse and Harrow, a thing he would never have dreamt of doing when he had the dead to consider. But for the rest of his new-found leisure-time, he busied himself with the shears. He finished his peacock, Opus One the Rector jokingly called it, and it looked less like a live peacock than one that had been stuffed by a bad taxidermist. Nevertheless, you could see the *idea*, as the Rector charitably said.

Autumn came, and the leaves fell everywhere save in Mr. Toombes's evergreen garden, where you could hardly tell summer from winter unless there was a sprinkle of snow. His topiary improved by leaps and bounds: the Artist coming out in him, as he himself put it. He did a rabbit with lop-ears, which was certainly lifelike although Miss Protheroe thought it looked pretty silly. And one November day when she complained about the owl that had kept her awake all night with premonitions of dying, Mr. Toombes said cheerfully:

"Owl in the yew? I'll do you an owl——"

And goodness, in almost no time it seemed, the yew-tree had become an owl-tree: it took the shape of that old bird that hooted horribly to the moon, most sinister and brooding and hunched against the first light snow. The real owl still hooted in Mr. Toombes's garden; and Miss Protheroe in her troubled dreams heard it, and wasn't quite sure whether it was live or in topiary. At dusk, if she went out into her garden to call in the cat, she would catch sight of the owl-shape, and it made her feel quite uncomfortable; it was an unneighbourly thing, gloomy and watchful, gazing over the boundary-fence right into the upstairs window which was bleared with steam when she had her bath twice a week, Tuesdays and Saturdays regular without fail. Once, as she was getting out of the bath, the real owl hooted triumphantly; scraggy and naked, she hurriedly wrapped herself in a towel.

It was just before Christmas, when that happened. Carol-singers were coming round, and Mr. Toombes would ask them into his parlour and pour out big glasses of parsnip wine and slap the young girls on their bottoms; but they didn't complain because after all it was the festive season. However, there were plenty of gossips to talk about the Goings On, after the next meeting of the W.I.; and a voice in Miss Protheroe's mind whispered: *Men, Men, Men, you can never be sure about them, and they get more like that, not less, as they grow older!*

Sometimes in her nightmares the yew-tree owl took on the features of Mr. Toombes and hooted at her incontinently.

Spring was in the air at last, and the girls and boys felt the stir of it and were up to goodness knew what in the bus-shelter from which Miss Protheroe had to avert her eyes as she passed it on her way home from the W.I. And as always in April the W.I. held its Annual Dance (*Husbands May Be Brought*) to which somebody lacking a husband brought Mr. Toombes, who insisted on dancing with all the younger wives. Miss Protheroe, whose thoughts were very refined even when they were top-secret whispers in her mind, paraphrased the things which the wives said at the W.I.: *He's got to the Age, you know. . . . It's something that happens to Gentlemen at his time of life.* But Gentleman or no, it wasn't very nice to think of Mr. Toombes as a next-door neighbour.

Soon spring was everywhere. Ignoring the NO HAWKERS notice on her gate, it crept into Miss Protheroe's garden with candytuft and mauve aubrietia and little dolly blue scillas and pale primroses dying unmarried. Next door the usual Dishonesty poked up its pink flowerheads through the clippings, the yew-owl brooded darkly, a cockerel stood on top of a cypress so lively-looking you could almost imagine it crowed, and Mr. Toombes's Opus One, the attenuated peacock, was pruned and trimmed and re-shaped altogether into a bird of the wildest fancy—a roc or a dodo or a phoenix bursting forth from the box-bush.

"It's the Artist coming out in me," said Mr. Toombes with pride, when people congratulated him on it. And now, as May brought out the naughty girls in their gay thin dresses, and the boys on their motor-bikes tearing up and down the lane, and the gypsies hawking clothes-pegs and taking no heed of the notice because they couldn't read —at this time of dismay for Miss Protheroe, who didn't like the spring because it was so Disturbing, Mr. Toombes next door sharpened his shears and set to work upon what was clearly intended to be his masterpiece. He began—very cautious, very conservative, like a sculptor with a precious

lump of marble brought all the way from Carrara—to trim
the two yews which stood on either side of his front door.

They were each about ten feet high; straight as soldiers,
but big-headed because of the Grecian vases which once
upon a time had surmounted them. These of course had
grown out of shape altogether; and among the tangled
twigs which composed them flocks of house-sparrows nested.
These came chirping forth alarmedly at the first clip-clip
of Mr. Tombes's shears.

For two or three days Mr. Toombes seemed content to
whittle away the outgrowing shoots without imparting any
particular shape to the yew-trees; indeed the Rector, jocular
as ever, called out, "What have you got there—Epstein's
*Genesis?*" Mr. Toombes took no notice. He went on clipping with immense concentration and did not address a
word to Miss Protheroe though she was weeding her flower-
bed within thirty yards of him. At noon, as usual, he went
up to the Horse and Harrow, from which he didn't return
until half past two. Immediately he mounted the step-
ladder and stood there, his vertigo quite forgotten, clipping
furiously throughout the sunny afternoon. Miss Protheroe,
as she knelt upon her lawn using an old dinner-fork to
prise out some intrusive plantains, heard him talking to
himself as he worked, rather incoherently; *The beer wag-
ging his tongue,* whispered her secret voice darkly. Not
much of it made sense (though she heard with awe the
names of Michelangelo and Leonardo da Vinci), but one
remark came to her clearly in a silence that fell between
the blackbirds' singing. It was one which she would remember later on.

"You got to be very careful in this lark," Mr. Toombes
admonished himself. "It's not as if you was a boy playing
with plasticine. Snip a bit off, you can't never stick it on
again. Easy does it, Mr. Leonardo."

Miss Protheroe retired into her cool cottage for tea, and nibbling a slice of her home-made seed-cake wondered about Mr. Toombes, and heartily wished she'd never set him off on his extraordinary hobby. But who would have thought that a man would become possessed by topiary, would let topiary turn his brain? On an impulse she went to the bookshelf and took down the *Encyclopædia of Gardening* and, looking it up under T, read the entry:

TOPIARY. *It is an old practice which has enjoyed a revival in recent years, but is not to be recommended for general use.*

She couldn't have agreed more; especially when she ventured out in the cool of the evening—Mr. Toombes had gone off to the pub—and she stared across her garden-fence at the two yew-trees, etched black in a sunset-shaft, standing tall above the heaps of clippings and the feathery sparrows' nests and the broken eggshells. Seeing them in profile, it suddenly dawned upon Miss Protheroe that the amorphous lumps of yew-tree were well on their way to becoming people. Two people. And already you could discern that the rough-hewn shapes were *not identical*. There was apparent in the upper half of the nearest figure a—a—Miss Protheroe scarcely dared define it to herself—*a swelling*. Or rather, *two* swellings. The figures, Miss Protheroe now realised, were to be of different sexes. A man and a woman were going to stand side by side at Mr. Toombes's front door.

This happened on a Friday. Next morning Mr. Toombes was at it early; she heard his shears going almost as soon as the birds started singing. She went out after breakfast, and emptied the cat-box as she always did after breakfast, and Mr. Toombes said an awful thing to her over the dividing fence—at least it seemed truly awful to Miss Protheroe:

"It makes you feel like God," he said, "making creature out of nowt."

Miss Protheroe didn't think it right that Mr. Toombes should liken himself to God; and squinting sideways, she was horrified to see the double tumescence now plainly manifesting itself upon the upper half of the nearest yew. She retreated into her cottage and stayed there until Mr. Toombes took himself off to the pub. Then she ventured out and squinted narrowly at the two figures. There was no doubt about it now: they had heads, shoulders, a suggestion of arms hanging at their sides. She stole out into the lane to have a peep at them from the front; but at that moment Mr. Toombes came back unexpectedly. The frenzy of creation must have dragged him early out of the pub. He tore up the steps, cast off his jacket, and took up the shears again. Feeling she ought to say *something,* since he had caught her peering at the figures, Miss Protheroe dared to say:

"In topiary . . . the . . . er . . . skirts and trousers . . . or perhaps I should say the draperies . . . are going to be rather difficult, aren't they?"

With terrible geniality Mr. Toombes leered at her over his shoulder.

"There won't be skirts and trousers; nor no draperies neither. These 'ere are Adam and Eve."

All the afternoon, as she made the rhubarb jam flavoured with ginger which she always made at this time of year, Miss Protheroe listened to him clipping. Towards evening she went upstairs and peeped out of a bedroom-window and saw that he had finished the woman and was at work upon the man. It was the man that worried her most. She couldn't see what Mr. Toombes was doing exactly, but she thought

he must be putting the finishing touches, for he walked
round and round the tree snipping very delicately here and
there. She pulled her curtain and went to bed; but she
couldn't sleep a wink as she tried to imagine, and tried
not to imagine, Adam and Eve standing on either side of
Mr. Toombes's garden-path next door. Now and then she
heard the owl hoot derisively. It was some time in the small
hours when she remembered that sinister remark of Mr.
Toombes's: "Snip a bit off, you can't never stick it on
again." It was then or thereabouts that she formed her
terrible resolve.

Johnny Williams the milkman was the only person, other
than Miss Protheroe and of course its creator, who ever
set eyes upon Mr. Toombes's Adam in its original, un-
bowdlerized state. At about half past seven he went up
Mr. Toombes's garden-path to leave his milk-bottle on the
doorstep as usual, and you could have knocked him down
with a feather. There was Mr. Toombes snoring peacefully
within the house, sleeping off the beer he'd had last night;
and there was the broom propped against the door where
he'd been sweeping up the last of the clippings; and there
was this Adam—well, who would ever have thought it?
"No, I'm not a-telling you," said Johnny to Mrs. Hanson, the next customer he called on, who happened to be
up and making a cup of tea. "Seeing's believing," he said.
"Just you go along and have a look!"
So Mrs. Hanson went along; but she had to change her
bedroom slippers for walking shoes and put on a warm
coat against the dewy chill of the morning; otherwise she
might have caught Miss Protheroe in the act. As it was, she
met her in the lane, scurrying back to her cottage as if the
Devil were at her heels. She was white as a ghost and trem-

bling, said Mrs. Hanson; and she was carrying a pair of shears.

As for Mr. Toombes's Adam—well, there was nothing special about it at all. Nothing like what Johnny Williams hinted he saw. Only a little tuft of twigs lying underneath it, on the garden-path which Mr. Toombes had swept clean last evening . . .

# Come Rain, Come Shine

More Country Contentments

John Moore

with drawings by Jennefer Porter

In this successor to *The Season of the Year* John
Moore reviews the pleasures, small and great, that
may be discovered within the pageant of the English
year. He finds beauty and interest in all the creatures
and events that regularly mark its progress. His
curiosity is never stilled whether he is contemplating
the ghastly ritual of the mating of spiders or recalling
the comic retreat homewards from a picnic on the
river, when 'There was a sense of urgency, as if the
mist were a poisonous miasma.' He writes of the
fantastic Squire Mytton, that wonderful eccentric
from the Brensham books who demonstrated his
contempt for paper money by letting 'a thousand or
two blow out of his coach on a windy night as he
came home from the races.' Cats, fishes, country
words, butterflies, the local flower show, all come
within the range of his special interest and observation. The author's feeling for country lore and
history, for the foibles and eccentricities of English-
men in their own countryside is implicit in every
word he writes.

ISBN 0 86299 103 X

**£4.95**

# A Cotswold Sketchbook

## Sir Alister Hardy

With text from *The Cotswolds* by John Moore

John Moore and Alister Hardy tramped the Cotswolds at more or less the same time and for more or less the same reasons – they both sought heartease, some quiet place where the unquiet heart might be at peace. Hardy, with sketchbook and paint-box, as a break from intensive scientific work; Moore, with pen, to escape too much London, debts, too many cocktails . . . The book of John Moore's journey was published as *The Cotswolds* in 1937 and is now very scarce. Sir Alister Hardy's watercolours and sketches accumulated over the years and have been left untouched since the artist left the position from which he painted them.

The two men never met but in this beautifully inspired and spontaneous collection of watercolours and sketches wrapped around John Moore's original text, here republished for the first time, a perfect marriage of words and pictures has occurred. The result will appeal to and inspire other artists, walkers, cyclists and all who love the Cotswolds.

ISBN 0 86299 126 9

£12.95

# A Boy in Kent

## C. Henry Warren
## New Introduction by
## Geoffrey R. Warren

C. Henry Warren belongs to that line of writers which includes H.E. Bates, Adrian Bell and John Moore. In *A Boy in Kent* he recreates the countryside of his childhood and his pages sparkle with supreme joy.

> We'll talk of sunshine and of song,
> And summer days, when we were young;
> Sweet childish days, that were as long
> As twenty days are now . . .'

This dedication, quoted from Wordsworth, sets the scene for what is to follow: a world of meadows and fields, the village pub and, in particular, the village shop, all seen through the eyes of a child. Everyone is a neighbour even though the village rambles over several square miles. A deep kindred spirit runs through its life and fills the pages of this vivid and beautiful memoir.

ISBN 0 86299 137 4

**£4.95**

# The Country of White Clover

## H.E. Bates

In the heat of a clear April morning in the
countryside somewhere between Valence and
Auxerre, H.E. Bates has the desire to stop the
flow of bursting bud, of fresh shoots, the
brilliance and richness and let it rest there.
Nothing of later summer could ever in any way be
more beautiful than this. By contrast, in England
more than half the beauty of spring is its length,
its long four-month course drawing out slowly,
uncertainly, with repeated moments of exquisite
and infuriating change.

These contrasts suffuse a book overflowing with
love for the countryside on both sides of the
Channel. A rustic world of trees and flowers, of
birds and animals, unfolding seasons and
characters such as Messrs. Kimmins and
Pimpkins; where every village contains its
Victorian survivor, man or woman, who has
never made a trip to even the nearest town and, in
typically stubborn or placid way, never wants to.

ISBN 0 86299 142 0

**£4.95**

Gloucester GL1 1HG

# The Linhay on the Downs
## Henry Williamson

Henry Williamson has that rare gift of making us see familiar things with a fresh eye, and unfamiliar things with a responsive eye. In *The Linhay on the Downs* he takes us both near and far, but we go nowhere without feeling that we are in the company of one who, as T.E. Lawrence said of him, 'could make even Bradshaw interesting.' He describes walks along the riverbanks and sea-coast of Devon, on Salisbury Plain, in London, in the Midlands and the Black Country. Then he takes us across the Atlantic, to New York, down to Georgia and Florida, up into New England and Canada, and home again to England.

The author tells of many places, people and animals – trout, turtles, alligators, white herons and rattlesnakes – always with a freshness and vigour that make this decidedly one of Henry Williamson's outstanding books.

ISBN 0 86299 194 3

**£4.95**

# The Lone Swallows
## Henry Williamson

*The Lone Swallows* was Henry Williamson's second book appearing first in 1922 and being enlarged and revised for the 'definitive edition' of 1933. Four stories appeared then for the first time including 'A Boy's Nature Diary', written in 1913 and thus the author's earliest recorded writing.

After the Great War, Williamson migrated to the Atlantic coast of north Devon where the sun was the only master and the only clock and where he was to pursue his writing career. At a rent of four pounds a year he moved into Skirr Cottage in the village of Georgeham full of zestful happiness. It was a village where a motor car arriving caused heads to crane from doorways and an aeroplane passing in the sky made dogs run for cover. He did not see a newspaper for a year and had an immense belief in the present and the future.

In that faraway time, from those faraway emotions, this book was composed. It is full of a love for the countryside and country people and was highly praised by J.B. Priestley. It is one of Henry Williamson's best books and will transport the reader to those Devon lanes of long ago.

ISBN 0 86299 193 5

**£4.95**

# Men and the Fields

Adrian Bell
with illustrations by John Nash

The drawings of John Nash perfectly match the country scene as described by Adrian Bell in this highly acclaimed portrait. In chronicling the life of the fields the author, with a sure touch and in beautiful prose, evokes a bygone world of farmers and shepherds, land owners and countrymen.

A new year's eve party in an old farmhouse yields a host of memories. As the year's hours grow fewer, the older people do the talking, the younger ones listen, and an England far older than the passing year is resurrected. One old lady tells of how the river was used for bringing chalk and coal to the farms. Another storyteller recalls how they used to go to Christmas parties in the country when he was a child. And so on, through the months of the year – the seasons unfolding in a highly personalised way as man and nature come together in a book to keep and to treasure.

ISBN 0 86299 136 6

**£4.95**

# A Country Scrapbook
## Lilias Rider Haggard

' . . . written with a feeling for the beauty both of things seen and of words in which to describe them . . .'  *Sunday Times*

'. . . characteristic of English writers on nature at their best . . .'  *The Listener*

'A book that everyone with the land's destiny at heart or in mind will want to buy and keep.'  *Punch*

'A delight from end to end, a book to go on the shelf of friendly and familiar volumes that we turn to again and again . . .'  *Country Life*

Lilias Rider Haggard knows about the countryside and what is more knows how to describe it – the people who live and work there, the day to day life in the villages and on the land, the colour of corn in wind, a kestrel's wings against a cloudless sky, the beauty of an old church. She sees with an artist's eye and in *A Country Scrapbook* has captured a moment of time which will long live in the memory.

ISBN 0 86299 170 6

**£4.95**